Praise for

Tears and Laughter and Happy Ever After

"This anthology has something for everyone. It's a delight. I only wish I was in it!"

Della Galton

"Like diving into a big box of Quality Street."

Kate Long

Tears
and
Laughter
and
Happy Ever After

Blot Publishing
2012

ISBN-13 9781900929080
ISBN-10 1900929082

First published in 2011 by Blot Publishing
www.blot.co.uk

A catalogue record for this book is available from the British Library.

This publication is also available on Kindle
ISBN-13 9781900929073
ISBN-10 1900929074

www.tearsandlaughter.co.uk
www.facebook.com/tears.laughter
twitter.com/tears_laughter

Tears and Laughter and Happy Ever After
is a vibrant and varied collection of stories from writers who between them have had hundreds of short stories published in women's magazines in the UK and around the world
(as well as other things in other places).

Thank you for joining us.
We hope you enjoy the ride!

Contents

A Single Strand of Spaghetti, A Single Drop of Olive Oil...

by Helen M Hunt

Food means everything to me. I see it as an art form, a journey, a quest for knowledge. I've been like this since I was a baby. My mother would sit me in a chair at the table and my unfocussed eyes would watch as she stirred a pudding or rolled a disc of flaky pastry.

Sometimes, as I got older, she would let me help her. I'd dip the moulting pastry brush in bright yellow egg and wash the tops of leaf-patterned pies for her. I'd press out round after round of scones, breathing in the cinnamon and nutmeg as they baked in the oven.

'You must always follow the instructions to the letter, Luke,' she would tell me as she used flour-doused fingers to turn the curling pages of whichever of her vast collection of cookery books happened to be open and propped up on the kitchen table between us.

I digested that advice at the time, but as I grew older, gained confidence and became my own chef, I realised it wasn't my style.

I preferred the chaos theory of cookery. A dash of this, a suggestion of that. Alchemy, love, nurturing, a blast of heat in the oven as a catalyst – and there you have it!

I've often wondered what she would have thought of the very last meal I cooked for her. The pies, the trifles, the finger food and the warming punch and port I laid on, that achingly cold day when we'd all stood around for what seemed like hours in the dark despair of St Peter's. As I handed round food and ladled out the warm fruit and cinnamon mixture embroidered with alcohol, I could feel her watching me from above.

My mother would never have dreamt of eating in a restaurant, of course. 'Why waste good money when you can cook something just as delicious at home?' she used to say. In the past I would have agreed – but that was before I discovered Valentino's.

Valentino's is a favourite haunt of mine. I love the checked tablecloths, the bottles of vinegar and oil on the table, the blinds at the window and the excited chatter from the kitchen.

'Ah! Luigi has made a perfect thin crust tonight!'

'Presto, presto, lots of hungry people out there!'

And Valentino. Of course, it's not his real name. In fact sometimes I think he's not even Italian. He's probably from Peckham, or Rochdale. But I go along with it, because I love his *Amore*-inspired accent, his shoes – which *are* Italian – and the way he wipes his moon-like forehead with a folded hanky.

He's on fine form tonight.

'Ah, Signor, your favourite table is free,' he says as he ushers me between the too-close-together tables and seats me with my back to the wall and a menu in front of me.

The menu talks to me like a long-lost lover. Spaghetti,

rigatoni, tagliatelle, ravioli, it whispers in hushed tones. Garlic, ground coffee and squeezed lemon all compete for the attention of my nostrils as I sit and think of Angela.

'How is your lovely lady?' asks Valentino as he deftly slips a glass in front of me and pours me my first Pinot Grigio of the night.

'Late as usual,' I laugh.

Ever since I've known Angela her timekeeping has driven me insane. I'm quite scatty, but at least I can tell the time. I even bought her a watch. A beautiful delicate one with a green strap and tiny emeralds set in the face.

'They match your eyes,' I'd said, rather cheesily, when I gave it to her.

She'd just smiled and kissed me.

Valentino frowns. He runs his hand through grizzled hair as he watches me.

'Will you order now? For both of you?'

'No. I'd better wait. She doesn't like me to make decisions for her.'

'I bring you antipasto.' Valentino grins and trundles off.

'Cheers mate,' I say, all Peckham-like. Valentino doesn't turn around.

I go back to the menu. They make all their own pasta here. They use their fingers to mix the silky cold flour and the sticky egg yolk together, lovingly coaxing it into a paste. Then they take the mixture and pass it through their tiny mangle-like pasta machine. The sheets of pasta get thinner and thinner and come out as glossy and smooth as Angela's skin.

They crush tomatoes in their fists and rip handfuls of herbs into the mixture to make their famous bolognese sauce. And the tomato paste smeared across their Pizza

Margherita carries all the plump satisfaction of Angela's lips when I kiss them.

I look at my watch. Half an hour since I arrived. Not unusual for her to be late though.

She floated down from heaven and into my life a year ago now. Angela: beautiful as Gabriel and scary as Beelzebub (for what is the devil if not a fallen angel?). Before Angela, all I had in my life was Valentino's, a shelf full of cookery books inherited from my mother and a hollow place inside that even the best pasta couldn't fill.

Then she came and shook me so hard out of my routine that I haven't stopped bouncing yet. She's a lot younger than me, but neither of us cares about that. She said she likes the fact that I've seen things she's only read about in history books. That she likes calling me 'old man' and laughing and that she likes the urgency of our kiss-sprinkled embraces.

Sometimes I wonder whether my mother would have approved of Angela. She'd have approved of me having a girlfriend. 'Settling down at last,' she'd have said. But, Angela... sometimes I think my mother would have been shocked by her vividness, her sense of the absurd, her language.

Valentino sweeps in and places a bowl of olives and some roasted peppers in front of me, along with a gingham-lined basket crammed with ciabatta and crunchy hard bread sticks. Olive oil sloshes across the peppers as I dip a piece of ciabatta crust. I watch as the olive oil is sucked up into its capillaries – juicy, green and tangy tasting.

In my mouth, it explodes with pepperiness. Like Angela when she is in a temper. I always try to kiss it better, but her dark hair and flashing eyes will not let me in when she is in that kind of mood. My love for her stretches beyond all reason, but she is unobtainable when she wants to be. And, oh, then the making up is exquisite.

Valentino's is never empty, yet it never seems to be busy either. Other couples chatter and kiss, some sit in frozen ice-bucket silence. Why do they come out together if they can't be bothered to talk? Why do they stay together if they have nothing left to say?

Angela always has something to say. Sometimes too much. Sometimes I have to hush her in whatever way I can so that she'll listen when I tell her things.

She did want to know about olive oil when I told her, about the virgin pressings. I had to put my finger on her lips to stop her giggling at that bit. About the olive groves, about cold pressing and warm pressing and blending. And she loved how messy we got when we fed each other spaghetti tossed in olive oil using just our fingers.

I wanted to take her to Italy and show her. I wanted to see the olives glowing like emeralds on the trees, smell the tomatoes ripening in the sun, feed each other grapes and fantasise about the wine they would be fermented into. 'Merlot, Valpolicella, Chianti,' I incanted over and over, trying to persuade her and make her share my dream. But Angela had a mind of her own, she wanted to go to Barcelona, so to Barcelona we went, for a holiday drenched in orange juice and fuelled by chorizo rather than lemon juice and salami.

Valentino is hovering again. 'Signor, would you like to order now?' He is anxious. Anxious to please. Not to offend.

'Okay,' I say. 'I'll have one spaghetti alla carbonara and one puttanesca.'

'And the lady won't mind?'

'No, she won't mind.' I hold up my glass for a top up.

Of course, I know she *would* mind. Nothing makes her eyes spark as much as being told what to do, or what to think.

I've had my fingers burned too many times not to learn that lesson. My angel has a red dress as well as a white one. I've never known a person to explode so quickly and so incomprehensibly.

'You don't understand,' she had screamed at me only last week. I hadn't even known what it was I was failing to understand. Perhaps that was the first time the age difference had mattered.

Valentino is acutely embarrassed when he arrives with two plates of food and she is still not here. He takes a hesitant half-step backwards just as I catch his eye.

'Never mind Valentino,' I say. 'It looks like I might be dining alone tonight.'

He places the plates in front of me with his usual practised grace, but he can't hide his discomfort and is clearly relieved to be gone.

The memory of Angela's words comes back to me. The last time I saw her.

'Stop trying to control me! You're not my father.' That bit had really hurt. I've never treated her like that. I'm not her father, she's not my daughter. She's my angel.

For once I don't enjoy my food. In deference to Valentino I eat both plates of food, but the carbonara and the puttanesca taste exactly the same. For the first time in my life, my taste buds refuse to show the slightest interest in Valentino's art.

I decline dessert. I'm not in the mood for the sharp tang

of lemon ricotta or the sensual delight of tiramisu. But Valentino gives me a glass of Muscat on the house and I take it out onto the wisteria-fumed verandah.

Sitting on the scrubbed pine bench, I throw back my head and look at the stars. Pinpoints of light – stars and angels – and then I hear her voice again.

'Look at me,' she sings, 'hold my hand and follow me.' She races across the sky, skipping around the Great Bear and into Orion's arms. The Plough does not get in her way and she traverses from the east to the west making a huge arc in the sky. Angela, my beautiful angel, flying and owning the sky.

And then, I realise she is no longer talking to me. She is talking to another angel. The stars sparkle and turn into forms so real I can almost reach up and touch them.

'Where am I?' Angela asks, as my heart breaks inside me. I want so much then to hold her hand and tell her what to do – whether she likes it or not.

Then an angel with wrinkles on her face steps forward. 'Come with me,' she says. 'I'll show you what you need to do. You don't have to work it out for yourself.'

'But,' says Angela, 'I've always worked everything out for myself. I don't need anyone to tell me what to do.'

Her voice is defiant, but her face is confused. I hold my breath so tightly it hurts as she turns towards the older angel and strains to hear her words.

'You must always follow the instructions to the letter,' she says, reaching out for Angela.

Angela hesitates and then takes the older angel's hand and goes with her. The tears that I have been holding back for days finally flow, pouring into my wine and diluting its sweetness. I'm no longer in denial.

All is quiet within Valentino's and I know I have come to the right place. Angela loved it here. This place cemented our relationship and fuelled it with the best food and drink that the world could offer. We spent all our happiest evenings here trawling everything on the menu from antipasto to dessert wine.

Where better than Valentino's to come on the day of her funeral?

How Deep Is Your Love?

by Cally Taylor

Oh my GOD. I think I can see Mike. I'm waiting on the platform and he's walking through the carriage of the train that's just pulled in, ducking his head. Gosh, he really is as tall as he said. I was worried about that. So many men on the internet claim they're six foot, but they're actually only five foot five and a bit. Why lie when it says on my profile that I'm five foot ten? It's not like I'm not going to notice.

Aw, he just let a little old lady go in front of him. How sweet is that? I fell in love with Mike the second I saw his profile on seekoutyoursoulmate.com. Actually that was probably lust, but it's definitely love now we've got to know each other properly. Not in the flesh, obviously, that's what this weekend is all about. Must. Not. Sleep. With. Him. On. First. Date.

We've exchanged thirty-eight emails and had fifty-two instant message conversations.

Is it sad that I know that? No phone calls though. Mike said he doesn't 'do' phone calls and he'd rather meet someone in person. I was a bit disappointed about that at first, but men don't really do three-hour chinwags with their mates, do they? They meet up in the pub instead. It doesn't matter though because we still know everything about each other.

I've memorised all his favourite films and bought a couple of his favourite CDs (hopefully my music collection won't look quite so sad now I've slipped Elbow and Granddaddy between my Abba and Shirley Bassey albums).

Oh, here he comes. He's stepping onto the platform and he's looking around and... Wow. He's SO gorgeous. He looks even better than his photos. Oh God. I hope he's not disappointed by how I look. My photos were totally up to date... well, from my holiday to Goa three summers ago. I was just a bit more tanned and a tad thinner then (it's amazing how much weight you can lose from dysentery). And my hair's shorter and not as blonde. No, it's fine. Mustn't start feeling insecure. He likes me just the way I am. He wouldn't have travelled all the way up from London to Nottingham if he didn't.

I wanted to go to London to see the place he shares with five other lads, but he said the house was a tip. 'I'm moving out soon anyway,' he said. 'No point you coming here.' Of course that meant I had to book Friday off work to tidy up *my* place. Not that we're going back there because I'm. Not. Going. To. Sleep. With. Him, but you know just in case... um... I take him back there for the guided tour before we go out to dinner. Or something.

He's seen me! He's smiling and waving at me. Gosh, is that his bag he's got over his shoulder? It's MASSIVE. It's like one of those army holdalls. Is he planning on visiting the launderette while he's up here? Doesn't matter. He looks really, really pleased to see me. Hooray, it doesn't matter that I'm fatter and paler than my photos. Thank God.

Okay, here he is.

Do I hug him or shake his hand? This is weird. I feel like I know him really, really well, but I've never met him before.

'Hi Sarah,' he says.

Wow, that was... kind of squeaky. He must be *really* excited to see me. And a hug. A really, nice, warm hug. And he smells good too.

'Shall we go for a drink?' I ask.

'Love to,' he squeaks.

Okay, this is really weird. Mike is as gorgeous as Johnny Depp, but he sounds like David Beckham on helium. We've been talking about his job for the last couple of minutes, but I feel like I'm talking to a 13-year-old boy.

'So I had to *fire* her,' Mike is saying. And I'm thinking, 'You're not old enough to fire anyone.'

He's twenty-seven and he's drop-dead gorgeous and he made me laugh loads during our instant message conversations, so why aren't I laughing now?

'Do you get it?' Mike says. 'So I had to fire her after she set off the smoke alarm. It was a joke.'

'Yes,' I say. 'Hee, hee.'

Oh no. This is really bad. I'm doing fake laughing. I *never* do fake laughing – not unless my boss is telling me a joke.

'By the way,' he says. 'Were you drunk when you emailed me last night?'

Shit. I'd totally forgotten about that. Last night I went out to dinner with my friends and had a totally miserable night. Everyone was coupled up and I felt like such a lonely, old gooseberry all on my tod. I got so drunk I could barely see when I got home, never mind type, but *somehow* I managed to put my fingers to the keyboard and type out an email to

Mike. I can't... exactly... remember what I said, but I think I wrote something about feeling like we had an incredible bond and that I couldn't wait to meet him. Don't judge me. I was a tiny bit emotional at the time.

'About what you wrote—' Mike squeaks.

'I'm glad you came,' I interrupt. 'Really glad you came.'

'Me too,' Mike says, squeezing my hand, and I feel a bit sick.

What's wrong with me? How can I not fancy someone with such beautiful high cheekbones and eyes the colour of Dairy Milk.

Okay, there's just one thing for it. I need to get really, really drunk.

'Another bottle of wine?' I ask.

Oh. Crap.

I just slept with him.

Don't judge me. I didn't *mean* to sleep with him, but I got the tiniest bit drunk over dinner and Mike said he should probably take me home. I thought he meant, 'I'll get the taxi to drop you home and I'll continue on to the station and go back to London,' but what he actually meant was, 'I'll get the taxi to drop us both back at your flat and then I'll kiss you on the back seat and you'll be so into it you'll invite me in.'

And I was. And I did.

The thing about Mike, you see, is that he's a really, really good kisser. And I haven't been kissed for ages – since Simon my ex, in fact. And I really wanted this date to go well. I told all my friends how this hot freelance record-producer from London was coming up to Nottingham for a date with me and they were all really jealous and, well, when he kisses me he doesn't talk.

Oh, Mike's rolling over. He's stroking my back. I like that.

'I haven't got any more condoms,' I say.

He starts kissing the back of my neck and my resolve not to sleep with him again starts to crumble. In fact, it totally disintegrates.

'I've got a sheath in my wallet,' he says, sliding his hand up and down my thigh. 'It's in my jeans pocket.'

I ignore the slightly creepy way he squeaks the word 'sheath' and reach for his jeans. Ah, there's his wallet. And there's the condom, in the little pocket bit, and his train ticket.

Hang on.

It's an open return. That's weird. Why didn't he buy a day return?

'Mike,' I say, but he kisses me before I can finish my question.

I open my eyes and stare blearily at the alarm clock beside the bed. 9.22am. Thank God it's Saturday. I can just go back to sleep and lie in until...

Oh God.

I slept with Mike last night, didn't I? Still, at least he's gone...

'Morning sleepy head,' he says, poking his head round the bedroom door. 'I thought I'd make you breakfast.'

He has too. He's carrying a tray towards me. There's a cup of coffee on it, a boiled egg in an eggcup and a slice of toast cut up into soldiers.

'Thanks,' I say, taking the tray. 'You shouldn't have.'

He *really* shouldn't have. What's he still doing here?

'Eat up,' he says, slipping into bed next to me. 'You're going to need the energy.'

I stare at him, my eyes wide. What does he mean by that?

We're *not* going to have sex again. I'm sober now and my head hurts. And he still sounds like a mouse that's been stepped on.

'Energy for what?' I ask nervously.

'For our trip to the park,' he says. 'You said in your email that there was this gorgeous park in the centre of Nottingham that you'd love to have a picnic in.'

'But,' I say. 'Don't you...'

I can't say it. I can't say 'Don't you have to go back to London.' That just sounds too rude. I can't sleep with him and kick him out. I don't want to be that kind of girl.

'You don't... want to mess up your nice leather shoes, do you?' I say finally. 'It rained loads yesterday and the park is bound to be muddy.'

'Don't you worry about that,' Mike says, bouncing off the bed. 'I've brought plenty of footwear.'

He delves into his enormous bag and pulls out a pair of trainers, a pair of hiking boots and a pair of cowboy boots. My stomach flips over, and not just because my eggy breakfast is making me feel a bit queasy.

'Hiking boots?' I say. 'You came well prepared, didn't you?'

We're halfway round the park and I'm trying to build up the courage to ask Mike when he's going back to London. He's holding my hand, swinging my arm back and forward, an enormous grin on his face. Oh God, he looks so damned happy.

'Mike,' I say, stopping by a bed of daffodils. 'Can I ask you something?'

'Of course, darling,' he says, gently stroking my cheek.

'Do you... have you... have you made any plans for tonight?'

That you need to get back to London for, I think.

'I do actually,' he says and my heart leaps with delight. 'I thought we could go to the cinema. My treat.'

'The cinema,' I repeat.

'That film is on,' he says, 'the romantic comedy you told me you wanted to see.'

He means the one I told him about in one of my emails.

'I was going to see that with my girlfriends,' I stutter. 'Tonight.'

Mike's grin fades slightly, but he brightens again just as quickly. 'No problem. You go and see the film with your friends and I'll cook a nice dinner for you for when you come back. You did say on MSN that you'd love to taste my Chicken Parmesan.'

'Yes,' I say, 'Yes I did, but...'

'Would you rather go out for dinner afterwards?'

'No, I just thought...'

'What did you think?' he asks, chucking me under the chin.

It's just one night. Just one more night and then he'll go back to London and I'll never have to see him again.

'Dinner would be lovely,' I say.

'That's great,' Mike squeaks, pulling me towards him for a massive hug. 'You said Nottingham was lovely and I wholeheartedly agree. I think it's much better than London.'

'You do?'

'Yes,' he says, kissing the top of my head. 'Oh and Sarah?'

'Yes,' I say, swallowing hard.

'My train ticket is valid for a month so I can spend some time with you before I collect the rest of my stuff.'

'What?'

'I wasn't sure about the question you asked in your email,

but now that we've spent time together I can honestly say that the answer is yes.'

'Which, er...' I cough. 'Which question was that?'

'You wrote: *You're so lovely, Mike. Do you want to spend the rest of your life with me?*'

The Day Before You Came

by Sally Quilford

The day before you came, Chloe didn't want to eat her cereal. She likes the milk warm, you see. Perhaps I should write that on my list, so that you know about it. My thoughts were elsewhere as I absent-mindedly poured the milk straight from the carton.

'No,' she said. 'No.' She realised my mistake before I did. I wondered if that was going to be the word for the day. No. She has days like that, when she picks one word and sticks with it. No is her favourite, but sometimes she'll say yes, whilst shaking her head, which can be a bit confusing. 'Bear' is another favourite word. And 'Pooh', meaning Winnie. She can sometimes say a few words together, but it's not always easy to make out what she's saying, so it can be a bit frustrating for her and for you. She's only a child, so you can't really get mad.

I think she knows something is going to happen. Early in the morning she crawled into my bed and touched my eyelid with her little finger. It's her way of seeing if I'm awake. Sometimes it's still dark, and hard not to feel snappy when tiredness is the first emotion you feel. So you'll try to understand that, won't you? She doesn't do it to be naughty. A 2-year-old doesn't know what naughty means. I'm preaching again and I know I shouldn't.

I almost didn't take her to nursery. I'd like to have kept her at home, so that I could enjoy the day with her. But she needs normality at the moment, to prepare her for the upheaval to come.

'It's your last day, Chloe,' said Rachel, the young nursery nurse. 'We're really going to miss you.' Chloe was already heading for the toy box.

'I don't think she realises,' I said.

'How are you feeling about it?'

'Wretched,' I said, straining to smile.

When I picked Chloe up later, Rachel handed me her daily diary sheet. I thought you'd like to know how she spent today so I wrote it alongside the list I'd made.

10am – Chloe enjoyed playing in the sandbox.

10.15am – Chloe painted a picture for her mummy.

10.30am – Chloe ate two slices of apple and half a banana.

10.45am – Chloe enjoyed sitting with her friends and hearing a story about Thomas the Tank Engine.

11am – Chloe had a nap in the quiet area.

My own morning read something like this:

10am–11.30am – Vicky wandered around the house, trying not to think about how empty it would be once Chloe was gone.

I took her into town for lunch. She likes the children's sandwich boxes they sell in the restaurant at the supermarket. Her favourite box has Winnie the Pooh on it, and comes with fruit instead of crisps. Not that she doesn't like crisps. I just try to ensure she eats healthily. I'm sure you'll do the same, won't you?

'Did you have a nice time at nursery?' I asked her. She

nodded as she pulled ham out of the centre of the sandwich and ate it. I wished at that moment she were a little bit older so she could tell me more about her day. The diary told me some of it, but I wanted to know her thoughts and her feelings as she did those things. I wanted something to remember. 'Aren't you going to eat some bread, Chloe?'

'No.' She smiled at me, mischievously, taking another piece of ham and folding it against her tongue.

'Please.'

'No.' She shook her head, giggling. 'No.'

It's important not to get angry with her when she does this. I know it's hard, when you want her to eat properly, but if you ignore it she will eventually eat the things you want her to. And I was right, because after I'd talked to her for a while, pointing out how nice Winnie the Pooh looked in the box, and saying how delicious her grapes looked, she picked up a slice of bread without really thinking. Only when she'd put it in her mouth did she look at me comically, as if to say 'oops'.

'You are a good girl.'

'No,' she said, but her head moved in that funny way she has, when she nods and shakes her head at the same time.

I know I shouldn't have spent money on the Tigger cuddly toy for her that afternoon. It seemed like I was buying her love, but I truly had intended to buy her a going away present. Oh, I know she's got the clothes I bought her, so you don't have to worry about that for a while, but I wanted... hoped... that when she cuddled up to Tigger, she'd remember I gave it to her. A pair of shoes or a pretty dress might not do the same trick.

After lunch, I took her to the park where we fed the ducks on her leftover bread. When she went on a swing I thought to myself, 'that will be the last time I see her do that', and when she went on the roundabout, I thought the same. When she flew across the grass and into my arms, like she always did when she was excited, I thought my heart would break. But no, it's still in one piece. It doesn't seem right really, because it should be cracked in two, what with a large part of it about to go away from me. I suppose we're made of tougher stuff than we think.

I kept her up later, even though I knew it would make her fractious in the morning, and that this might cause problems for you. I had to savour those moments with her, the day before you came, as I'd never have those moments again.

When she was in bed, I said to her, 'Are we going to practise saying it? I love you, Mummy.'

It's so funny when she tries to do it, clumsily forming her lips around the words 'love' and 'you', so that they come out 'woo woo'. One day she'll say it and know what it means.

I've finished the list of all the things she likes and dislikes. Along with the things she likes one day, but not the next. Children are like that, and it's important you know, so that you don't get angry with her when she goes through these changes.

There I go preaching again. I know everyone deserves a second chance. The girl who gave birth to someone as precious as Chloe certainly does. So when you come and take her away from me tomorrow, please make the most of that chance.

As I watched her sleeping, for the last time, I wondered if I could do this again. But I know that when the fostering agency rings me and offers me another Chloe, or another Jack, or another Ben or another Paige, I'll take them and love them as I've loved her. Because children like Chloe deserve a second chance too.

The One that Got Away

by Karen Clarke

I bumped into him in the chemist's of all places, on a chilly autumn day.

'Angie! Is it really you?'

The hairs on my arms stood on end. It was as if we only parted yesterday – or never parted at all – and my heart began pounding.

'Calum!' I spun round flustered, hot colour flooding my face as I backed into the perfume counter. 'What a surprise!'

He registered my shock with amusement and his trademark grin.

'I've just moved back,' he said, with a trace of American drawl. He curled a hand against my cheek and the unexpectedness of it snatched my breath away.

In snapshots, I noted the fine lines on his forehead and how his tan darkened his eyes to charcoal. 'The company relocated,' he elaborated, eyes drinking me in, and I wished I wasn't wearing tracksuit bottoms and had some make-up on.

'Still working at the old place?'

I nodded, the imprint of his hand scalding my cheek. 'Day off.'

'It's so good to see you, Angie.' Desire threaded his words

and my mind tumbled back to the intensely passionate year we spent together, before his promotion took him abroad and away from me. 'I think about you a lot.'

Why did you go? I wanted to cry. *Why didn't you come back, like you promised?*

So many times I've rehearsed what I would say, but the words got stuck in my throat and I swallowed them down.

I still couldn't comprehend how such longing, such fire could have been so easily extinguished.

'He's a player,' colleagues warned from the start. 'He was sacked from his last job for sleeping with the boss's wife.'

But I knew I was different, knew in my soul he felt what I felt and believed him with every fibre of my being when he said we'd be together forever.

'I was an absolute idiot to let you go,' he said softly, as if we were the only people in the shop and that's how it felt, everything receding and dwindling until it was just the two of us.

Calum was the one that got away. The biggest challenge of my life had been getting over him, but already I was weakening, remembering the heat of his lips, his arms, his breath on the nape of my neck.

'Are you married?' His eyes flicked to my hands in their old-fashioned woolly gloves and I quickly shook my head.

'You?' My teeth clattered and I clamped my lips together.

'No.'

Elation pushed through me. He'd saved himself – for me. I wanted to laugh and cry and press myself against him.

'Can we meet later?' he said, eyes honing in on my lips and I was nodding before the words were even out of his mouth. 'We can talk properly, catch up,' he added, and I carried on nodding foolishly.

His lips grazed my cheek like a promise. 'Seven o'clock?

There's a place on Church Street where we...'

'... used to meet every Friday night after work,' I finished in a rush, happy he'd remembered. 'It's still there.'

He grinned. His teeth flashed too white against his tan and suddenly, briefly, he was a stranger. Someone I didn't know at all. 'I can't wait,' he murmured, and I turned and dashed into the street, noise filling my ears as if someone had turned the sound up.

I was smiling like I hadn't in ages. I thought, I should buy something new to wear. Get my hair done properly, but there wasn't time.

There wasn't time. My smile faltered.

I glanced at my watch and quickly headed to the car-park. I was already running late, distracted from my normal routine by the need to buy toothpaste. It must have been fate that drew me to the chemist's, pulling me there like a magnet.

I didn't even buy any in the end; I would have to call at the supermarket later.

I fumbled my car-keys out of my bag and as I slipped into the driver's seat, a smile still hovering round my mouth, I saw him again, standing by a red Porsche at the other end of the car-park. My heart leapt into my throat.

His arm was hooked round the waist of a tall woman with long, fair hair, and she was laughing up at him with the easy intimacy of someone who knew him well.

I slid down in my seat as he looked round, my stomach cramping with shock. Reality crashed in.

How could I have been so stupid? He hadn't changed at all. Not one bit. He probably saw me in the street and followed me. I imagined him inventing some brilliantly plausible excuse for the woman's benefit.

When he left for America, my boss let slip that Calum was

seeing someone else behind my back. I hadn't believed it then, but seeing him now, cupping a hand round the woman's neck and drawing her in for a kiss, I suspected he'd been right.

Cheeks wet, I roared past them – noting with grim satisfaction the shock in his eyes when he realised it was me.

I felt sorry for the woman. I wondered if she knew and turned a blind eye, or trusted him with her life, like I had.

Children were tumbling out when I arrived at the school, their arms outstretched, and shrieks of laughter streaming out behind them.

'Mummy, you're late,' cried Lottie, flinging herself at me, forgetting to be cool like her friends.

'Come here you.' I pulled her close, my world swinging sharply into focus. For a few crazy minutes I'd envisaged a completely different future for us, but hadn't considered her at all.

Suddenly I was fiercely glad I wasn't that girl any more – naïve and trusting to the point of being blind, forsaking friends and family for a man who couldn't care less.

'Can we go to the park, Mum?' Lottie was swinging her rucksack, her dark eyes – so like Calum's – dancing merrily. His loss, I thought. *His loss.*

'Please, Mummy, please?'

I smiled at her, a space opening up in my mind where Calum had been lurking like a ghost for far too long. 'Of course we can,' I said bending down again, removing my gloves to help her on with her coat.

My wedding ring caught the light, and shame prickled my skin.

'Not for too long, though,' I said, zipping her up tight and kissing the tip of her nose. 'I'm planning a very special dinner tonight, when Daddy gets home from work.'

Communication Breakdown

by Sarah Dunnakey

It was a Tuesday. I know that for a fact, because it was the day after the ice-cream van blew up. And that was definitely a Monday.

Jim and I always have a choc-ice ice each after tea on Monday, and that week we had to do without. I told him he should have nipped out as soon as we heard the tune. He could have been there and back before it blew. Not that that would have helped poor Mr Bernelli, but at least we'd have had our pudding.

Jim said he didn't really miss it. Said he'd never really liked choc-ice ices anyway. I told him not to be so daft.

So, a Tuesday, definitely. It started normal. Except for the ice cream van debris in the road. And the police vans. And that stripy tape stretched everywhere.

Joan had asked me to call in on my way to the shops. I filled her in on the latest news, but she was ever so distracted. Didn't seem to take in that the neighbourhood had lost its ice cream supply for the foreseeable future. Kept talking about lights in the sky.

'That'll have been the ice pops,' I said. 'Went shooting up like rockets they did. And there's a lake of Magnums on the tarmac. The cats think it's Christmas.'

'Shut up Alice.'

That's what she said. Her exact words. Never spoken to me like that before. Not even after that time with her Nigel and the mistletoe.

'Just shut up,' she said again. There was a wobble in her voice. 'This is important. You have to listen.' She got up and pulled the curtains closed. Which was a shame, because it was a lovely day.

'I haven't got much time,' she whispered.

'I know. Half-day closing,' I whispered back. 'But if we get going now we should just catch the butcher's.'

'No! Listen,' she said. She was chopping her hands about and her jaw looked so stiff I thought she'd got a cramp. I've always thought her living room was a bit sparse, lots of pale wood and white cushions. Not enough ornaments. I was glad of it then as she paced about, arms a-flailing. If we had been at mine I would have feared for my china.

She stopped suddenly. 'You haven't heard a word I've said, have you?'

'Lights,' I said, remembering that bit. 'In the sky. Government spy satellites?'

Joan sighed and sat down. 'I've seen them five nights in a row. Like fairy lights they are. Pretty, I thought, when I first spotted them. But now...' She pulled the edges of her cardigan closer across her chest. 'That ice-cream van wasn't the first.'

'I'm pretty sure it was,' I protested. 'Mr Bernelli's been here since the sixties. He started in that kiosk on the seafront. Do you remember? Your Nigel bought me a 99 there once. Don't know where you were. Happy times.'

Joan reached out and grabbed my hands. Her fingers were cold.

'Not the first explosion,' she said, speaking so slowly that I watched her lips form each word. 'There have been others.'

Her fingers were holding mine just a bit too tightly and I wondered if maybe it had been a mistake to mention Nigel and the 99.

'And that's not all. The old red phone box on Albert Street. Disappeared three days ago. Into thin air. I rang the council, but they said it was nothing to do with them. And the traffic lights on the High Street yesterday. Started flashing pink and blue. Caused chaos in the centre of town. Then there's Mrs James at the newsagents. Or rather there isn't. Not anymore. Gone. Mr James is devastated.'

'He would be,' I interrupted. 'He'll be having to get up to do the papers himself. Horrible job on a cold dark morning.' Her grip on my hands tightened.

'I think I'm going to be next,' she said. 'They know I've been watching them. They're focussing in on the house.'

'Is it the television licence people?' I asked. 'They've got these special vans you know.' I'd seen it on an advert. Very impressive. Wouldn't have put Joan down as a fee-dodger. But you never know. 'Have you not got a licence?'

'You haven't been listening to a word have you?' she said.

I shook my head. Then nodded. Then shook it again.

She let go of my hands at last and sank back into her chair.

'There are things up there,' she said. She was staring at the ceiling. I looked up too. There was a nasty brown patch in one corner where their shower had leaked last year.

'You need to get Nigel onto that,' I said. 'Bit of emulsion

would do the trick.' He was good with DIY was Nigel. Many a time I'd got him over to do those jobs that needed a tall strong man. He could always be persuaded to stop afterwards for a cup of tea and a slice of my lemon drizzle. I told Jim we were lucky to have him. Although lately when I'd rung he'd been too busy, sometimes so busy he hadn't even answered the phone.

Joan leaned forward suddenly and I flung my hands behind my back, just in case she was thinking of grabbing them again.

'Come on Alice. Lights in the sky. People disappearing. Things exploding.' She let out a sharp breath. 'Don't you watch television at all?'

'Of course I do. But nothing like that's ever happened on Come Dine With Me.'

'Aliens,' Joan said. And her eyes went all big and goggle-like. There was a pause. I got the feeling she was waiting for me to say something.

'Film?' I suggested. 'That lovely woman with the name I can never pronounce? Shaved all her hair off. Oh!' I clutched my stomach. 'That nasty skittering monster thing.'

I looked at the ceiling again. Something up there? Skittering? 'Could be squirrels.' I said. 'They make a horrible racket if they get in your roof. Send Nigel up with a broom.'

'Not squirrels. Not the television licence people. Not monsters.' Joan's voice was calm and matter of fact now. She folded her hands neatly on her lap, as if she was about to address the Parish Council.

'It's aliens,' she said. 'And I think it's their way of saying hello.'

I wondered if I should ring Nigel. Tell him he needed to

come home early. That Joan was having a 'turn'.

'I think it's a problem with translation,' she continued. 'A misunderstanding. We can't interpret their flashing lights, but they think we're not listening properly. So they're having to shout. The explosions, the disappearances. Trying to get their message through.'

She looked at me for a moment and then stood up. 'Sorry, but I've got to go, I'm meeting Nigel at the station.' She glanced at her watch. 'We're off to Scotland on a mini-break. A lodge by a loch.' She smiled. 'He booked it as a surprise and his timing couldn't have been better.'

She was looking at me again now with what a less polite person than myself might have called a stare. 'A romantic holiday for an old married couple who still love each other very much.' Another smile. 'Misunderstandings, Alice. People getting the wrong end of the stick. It happens all the time.'

As she moved towards the door she called back, 'No need for you to go just yet though. Just drop the latch on your way out. There's some food in the fridge that won't last 'til we're back. You help yourself. Take your time.'

'But I thought you said we didn't have much time,' I said.

Joan sighed. 'You really should listen more carefully Alice. I said *I* didn't have much time.' She looked at her watch again, called 'Have fun!' and was gone.

I headed for the kitchen. I was sure the fridge would be full of treats. I'd bumped into Nigel in the supermarket at the weekend. I definitely spotted salmon and cream cakes in his trolley. I tried to persuade him to stop for a coffee, but he said he was in a hurry, almost barging into me as he headed for the till. There'd been a couple of fancy quiches in there too. I opened the fridge door.

There was a bright white light. Not from the fridge, from everywhere but the fridge, from all around. The floor started shaking and then the house, with me in it, was spinning up and up and up.

Joan was right. They're not monsters. They're not even green, which was a bit of a disappointment. I tried to explain that to their leader. Even drew some pictures of what aliens should look like. I think he got the idea. He nodded, and studied it for a full minute, before vaporising it.

They've shown me their plan. A big scribbly thing in 3-D, like a Christmas decoration made from coat-hangers, with a shiny bluey-green bauble hanging below. Think I've got my head round it now, with a bit of help from the captain and much pointing and waving between the wires and the small blue ball. Looks like Joan was right. They want to make contact with Earth. Like she said, they were only trying to say hello, have a bit of a chat. They just haven't learned the finer points of conversation yet. But it's okay, now I'm on hand to help I'm sure there'll be no more misunderstandings. The planet has never been in safer hands.

We'll Meet Again

by Kathleen McGurl

Kelly was wearing a new brooch. A large amber, surrounded by marcasite, set in gold-coloured metal. Nice, but rather old-fashioned for a seventeen-year old, I thought.

'That's pretty, love,' I told her.

'Got it off eBay,' she said, fingering it proudly. 'It's 1930s. I like this old stuff.'

Kelly had recently discovered eBay. She'd sold her old Barbie dolls on the online auction site, and then she'd bid for some DVDs which she'd got for a fraction of the shop price. Now she'd begun looking at costume jewellery and clothes. It was a good way for her to spend some of the money she earned from her Saturday job.

But lately, everything she bought was vintage – from the 1930s or 1940s. I supposed she was trying to forge a new style for herself. Girls of that age like to be different from the crowd.

'It's just a phase,' Mike said, when I talked to him about it. 'And rather vintage than punk, I say.'

Her next purchase was a 1940s tea dress. It was made of flowered cotton, had a Peter Pan collar and mother-of-pearl buttons. Lovely – in a museum-piece kind of way. I wondered if she was turning into a collector, but she began wearing the dress around the house, changing into it as soon as she got home from college.

'It feels right, Mum,' she said. 'Like it goes with the house.'

We'd moved into the house about a month before. It was a pre-war house, packed with original features. We'd inherited it from my spinster great-aunt Betty, who'd lived here all her life. My grandmother, now eighty-six and in a retirement home, hadn't wanted us to move in.

'There's something strange about that house, you know,' she'd warned. 'There are things you don't know about. Things that happened a long time ago. You want to be careful, in that house. There's a *presence* there.'

'Don't be silly, Gran,' I'd said. 'You grew up there. It can't be that bad. And I don't believe in ghosts.' But Gran had pursed her lips and refused to say anything more.

Over the next few weeks, Kelly acquired more vintage clothes, and began wearing them all the time.

'I like them, Mum,' she said. 'In any case, that's all I can find on eBay these days.'

'What do you mean?' I said. 'There's loads of contemporary stuff.'

'Not for me,' Kelly replied. 'Come on, I'll show you.'

She went to the computer and opened up eBay. I watched her set up a search for women's clothing. A page appeared showing thumbnail photos of items, with brief descriptions alongside.

'There you are, you see,' I said. 'Those are all modern things. Look at that lovely leather jacket! And that gorgeous dress from Monsoon!'

Kelly just looked sideways at me, then clicked on the

Monsoon dress. But the page which opened up showed something completely different – a plain, pale yellow blouse with a rounded collar and set-in sleeves. *Genuine 1940s blouse*, said the details. *Some repairs to hem, but otherwise perfect condition.*

'Hmm, I like that one,' Kelly said, dreamily. 'It would go with my navy skirt.'

'Love, you haven't got a navy skirt,' I said. Kelly shook her head and looked at me, her big brown eyes filled with worry.

'I know I haven't, Mum. But *she* has.'

'Who's she?' I asked, but Kelly stood up and went to her bedroom without replying. I sat down at the computer and clicked the Refresh button. The yellow blouse disappeared, and in its place was a photo of the Monsoon dress.

'Kelly,' I called. 'Come and look at this – I'll pay for it if you'd like it.' I wanted my twenty-first century girl back again – jeans and all.

Kelly came back downstairs wearing one of her forties frocks. She'd pulled her hair back into a thick hairnet at the nape of her neck. 'Mum, call me Joan, please, from now on. I hate the name Kelly.'

The next day she refused to go to college. 'It seems so indulgent, Mother. Wasting my time studying literature when all those poor souls are suffering. I want to do something more important with my time.'

'Like what, Kelly?'

'Joan. I asked you to call me Joan. I don't know. Maybe I can get a job driving ambulances. Or in the munitions factory.'

She spent the day knitting socks. When Mike came home we had a whispered conversation in the hallway.

'I'm worried, Mike. This isn't just a phase. It's more like – I don't know – like she's possessed.'

'Possessed – that's a strong word, Ali. By whom?'

'Joan, whoever she is. Or was.'

'Did someone call my name?' Kelly said, coming out of the living room. 'Oh hello, Father. I'm glad you're home safe, and before the blackout begins.'

'Blackout?' said Mike. 'Father? I'm your *Dad*, Kelly. And this nonsense has to stop. Wearing all these ancient clothes and acting as though there's a war on. It's 2011, for goodness sake! And you'd better not miss any more days at college, or you'll never pass those exams.'

Kelly just stood, head bowed, hands clasped in front of her while he spoke. When he finished, she nodded meekly. 'Yes, Father.'

At the weekend, Kelly asked if she could move her things into the spare room. 'This was always my room, Mother. It's full of happy memories for me.'

'We've only lived here two months, love,' I said.

'But I've always been here,' she replied. 'I was born here. So were my sisters, Margaret and Betty.'

I felt a cold shiver run down my spine. Margaret was my grandmother. Betty was my great-aunt who'd left us the house. But they hadn't had a third sister – that I knew of. My grandmother's words came back to me – *there are things you don't know. Things that happened. A presence, in the house.*

I resolved to ask Gran about Joan. Maybe I'd take Kelly with me.

'That's a pretty dress, dear,' Gran said, when we arrived at the home. 'My sister used to have one just like it.' Kelly was wearing her 1940s flowered tea dress.

'Your sister, Betty?' I asked.

'No, er, yes. That's right. My sister Betty.'

Normally I'd have assumed Gran's uncertainty was down to her age, but now I wasn't sure. Was she hiding something?

'Gran,' I asked. 'Who was Joan?'

'Where did you hear that name?' she snapped.

Kelly stared at her. 'It's my name, now.'

'It's not your name. Though you are very like her, especially in that dress,' Gran said.

'Like who, Gran?'

'Her. Joan.' She sighed. 'I suppose it won't hurt to say, now Betty's gone. Joan was our other sister. She died, during the war.'

'Oh Gran, how sad! Why did you never talk about her?'

'Betty didn't want me to. Joan killed herself, you see. She was only seventeen. My parents and Betty were ashamed – there was a stigma attached to suicide in those days, you know.'

'The poor girl,' I said, glancing at Kelly. She was white. 'Why... why was she so unhappy?'

'She'd had a sweetheart. His name was...'

'Jack McBride,' finished Kelly. Gran and I turned to look at her, open-mouthed.

'How did you know that?' Gran asked.

'He was tall, dark haired and dimpled,' Kelly said, staring at the wall, focussed on something only she could see. 'We were going to marry.'

Gran spoke quietly, watching Kelly. 'Joan had promised to marry him, on his next leave. And our parents had given their consent. But poor Jack...'

'...never made it back. He was killed on the Normandy beaches, on D-Day. Deliverance Day!' spat Kelly. 'Death Day, more like.'

'She's right,' whispered Gran. 'And Joanie was so angry. Just like Kelly is now. It's as though – as though Joanie's come back to us, in Kelly.'

'I have come back, Margaret,' said Kelly, taking Gran's hands in hers. 'I'm here.'

'But,' I gasped, 'where's Kelly? Where's my daughter?'

'She's here,' Kelly, or Joan, said. 'We're, well, sharing her body, I suppose.'

'But Joanie,' Gran said. 'Kelly's young, she has her life ahead of her. Leave her be!'

'I had my life ahead of me too,' said Joan, bitterly. 'Till Churchill sent my Jack to die on the beaches. I killed myself to be with him. But I can't find him, Margaret. I can't find him!' She buried her face in her hands and sobbed. My heart went out to her. Kelly hadn't cried like that since she was a little girl. And no 17-year-old in love should have to lose her fiancé like that.

'Joan,' I said. It felt so strange to call my daughter by that name. 'Is that what you want? To find Jack again?'

She looked up at me, her eyes ringed black with tear-stained mascara. 'Yes,' she said. 'That's all I want.'

I'd had an idea.

Mike thought it just might work. 'We have to resolve this somehow, Ali,' he said. 'We want our vibrant young Kelly back. And a holiday in France isn't a bad idea, in any case.'

A few days later we took the car ferry to Le Havre. I'd spent a few hours on Kelly's beloved computer, which she hadn't touched since Joan had taken over, researching the D-Day landings. I'd found out where Jack's company had been sent, and where the casualties had been buried. Finally I'd struck lucky, and the Commonwealth War Graves

Commission website had given me the information I needed.

It was about an hour's drive from Le Havre to Banneville-la-Campagne. The cemetery was just 100 metres from the main road. We parked the car, then Mike twisted round to speak to Joan.

'Now, do you know why we're here?'

She nodded, slowly. She'd been quiet for the whole journey. I wasn't sure if she was looking forward to finding Jack, or dreading it. Perhaps she didn't know herself.

'Come on, then,' Mike said, and we all got out of the car. I helped Gran out, and handed her her walking stick. She'd insisted on coming with us.

'She's my little sister, Alison. This might be difficult for her, and I want to be there for her.'

We made our way slowly past the rows of white crosses, each one marking a story as tragic as Jack's. And for each Jack, there could be a Joan. All those wasted and ruined lives. I silently prayed for them as I passed each grave.

And there he was. Plot D673. A white cross, like all the others, surrounded by neatly tended lawn. The only difference between this and the thousands of others was the name inscribed into the stone. Captain Jack McBride, June 6th, 1944.

Joan gasped. 'Jack, oh my Jack!'

Gran caught hold of her arm. 'His body's here, Joan. Is he here, for you?'

Joan turned to her sister with shining eyes. 'He's here, Margaret. And he's waited for me! I've found him, after all these years!'

The two sisters hugged each other – one frail and old, the other a teenager. 'Goodbye, Joanie,' said Gran. 'Go to him, now.'

'Goodbye, Mags. And thank you,' she said, turning to Mike and me. It was an awkward moment. Did we say goodbye too, to our *daughter*?

While we hesitated, a faint mist rose up from Jack's grave. For a moment I thought I saw the outline of a tall man, in uniform. The mist drifted towards Joan, enveloped her, then dispersed, as quickly as it had formed.

Kelly shook her head and blinked. 'Mum, I really hope you've brought some decent clothes for me to change into. I am *so* sick of these blinking dowdy frocks.'

'Kelly! You're back!' Mike and I both rushed to hug her.

Gran was crying quietly into her handkerchief. 'Good to have you back, young Kelly,' she said, kissing her great-granddaughter's cheek.

'Of course I've brought some clothes, love!' I said. 'Come on, they're in the car.' I'd secretly packed jeans, a t-shirt and her favourite Ugg boots she'd found on eBay before Joan took over. Mike and I each took one of her arms, and we walked, laughing and chatting, towards the car park.

I glanced back, to see Gran still standing for a moment longer at the grave. We'd regained a daughter, but she'd lost a sister, for the second time. When the time came, I'd bring her ashes here, to scatter where she'd be able to find her sister once more.

The List

by Bernadette James

The crack had started months ago. It had begun as nothing more than a fine line at the upper corner of the room where the wall met the ceiling, barely noticeable, but over time it had lengthened and expanded to a ragged crevice that could no longer be ignored.

Sarah looked at her list and considered where this latest fault should be positioned. It was certainly more important than the peeling wallpaper in the spare room. That was surely only cosmetic. What about the leak from the shower? They could live with that a while longer, at least until it started to seep through the decaying grouting where it could cause more damage. It was only for guests anyway and they didn't have many of those anymore. The water that poured in under the back door was a more urgent problem. The linoleum tiles in what passed for a utility room looked as though they were starting to swell and lift due to the excessive moisture and Sarah didn't want to add flooring to her list as well.

She inserted 'cracked wall' below 'back door' and above 'shower' and tried to avoid thinking about what might have caused it.

Sarah had had her doubts about buying this house. Despite its pretty garden and delightfully quirky layout, its age indicated that it would take a lot of looking after. Andrew had assured her that they could cope with it and that it would be worth all the effort. He had neglected to mention that the effort involved would all have to come from her.

Nevertheless, she had allowed her fears to be allayed and had been swayed by the obvious charms of the property. The sash windows, the roll top bath, roses rambling across the front of the house and around the walled garden, the lavender – they had all played their part in persuading her.

Ten years on she didn't see them anymore. She saw mould, blocked sewers and chimneys that needed re-pointing. She saw ancient boilers, warped doors and broken roof tiles. And now she saw cracks in the walls as well.

It was impossible to keep on top of it all. When they had first moved in she had carefully gone round the property and noted the things that needed fixing. Some of those things were still there, on the list to which she had just added the cracked wall. It wasn't the same list physically, of course. Items had been added and crossed off over the years and the list had been rewritten many times. It persisted in getting longer despite her best efforts.

Tradesmen! Where had all the good ones gone? They didn't return your calls, they never turned up when they were supposed to, they took twice as long and cost twice as much as they had originally estimated (old properties were hard to judge, apparently) and more often than not they made things worse rather than better. The engineer who was hired to fix the central heating had succeeded in bursting the cold water tank which then leaked through the sitting room ceiling. The en-suite bathroom – their biggest project and expenditure – had never been without fault, owing to the antiquated plumbing. It was a Herculean task.

Andrew didn't understand why it was such an issue. If there was a problem, you called someone and they fixed it. He had to work long hours to pay the mortgage. Surely Sarah could take responsibility for a little bit of house maintenance. Was that too much to ask?

They had argued and it had got quite nasty. Andrew said that Sarah moaned all the time and didn't appreciate what he did for her. Sarah said that Andrew was never there and had dumped all of the house problems on her. Andrew said if she hated the house so much why didn't she go and live somewhere else. Sarah had said she might just do that. There were some nice new flats on the other side of town and they could afford one each if they sold up.

Everyone had rows and people said things they didn't mean, Sarah knew that. Nevertheless, she didn't discuss the house problems with Andrew anymore. It was clear that she was on her own with this. Anyway, she was no longer sure that she hadn't meant what she said.

Sarah looked again at the list she still held in her hands. She couldn't face it. She couldn't face any of it. What had happened? Her life had become an incessant round of building problems and arguments. Her home and her marriage had both shown their true colours. There had to be more than this.

She took the list in both hands and tore it with venom into two ragged pieces, then four, then eight. She let the remnants flutter to the floor and picked up the phone to call the estate agent.

Andrew had chosen to be absent when the agent called. He had gone to play golf, telling Sarah that it was her idea and she could deal with it.

The man who came was, unsurprisingly, not the same one who had sold them the house. Sarah had been apprehensive about the visit, hoping that there wasn't too much discussion of defects and imperfections that would lower the asking price, but her worries were unfounded.

The young agent gasped at the cornicing, salivated over the original fireplaces and almost fell to his knees and wept when he saw the garden. He went from room to room, scribbling constantly in a little book.

Sarah began to feel guilty. She didn't want to deceive anyone and would hate to think that, in another ten years, there would be another woman feeling as trapped as she did by the responsibility of this property.

She began to point out the flaws in the house: the cracks, the leaks, the badly fitting doors. The agent didn't seem to hear her. She told him that they could only flush the toilets twice a day because of the sewers, but he carried on oblivious to her comments, continuing his rapturous praise. Finally, when she commented on the immense quote they had had for replacing the sash windows he had turned to her with a slightly exasperated expression and told her that he could see the faults himself, thank you. It was his job, after all.

He showed her his notebook, where he had jotted down many items similar to those that had been on her own list. Against each room, there was at least one thing that needed work, a niggle, a problem. She opened her mouth, about to tell him that he needed to point these out to any potential purchaser, it was only fair. But he held up a hand and directed her to the rest of his list, where he had written down the good things, the quirkiness, the charm.

There were many, many more things there.

He assured her that they were an honest agency, that no one would be misled into thinking it would be easy. Nevertheless, he was confident that the house would sell itself. It was unique, a one off, a home. Things came in packages, he told her. Nothing was perfect. He promised to be in touch soon.

Sarah stood at the door and watched him leave. It was a bright day and the sun had warmed the lavender flowers, persuading them to share their calming scent. A ladybird was making its way up the stem of a rose, hungry for greenfly, nature's own solution. The redbrick walls glowed behind the abundant foliage. It was a lovely garden, Sarah had to admit.

She went inside and wiped her feet on the mat that covered the original terracotta tiles, each one slightly different, like snowflakes. She wandered down the crooked passages, through almost hidden doorways, into every corner of the house, looking, really looking, trying to see what the estate agent had seen, what she and Andrew had seen ten years earlier. Yes, the wall was cracked, but the picture rail was beautiful. Yes, the windows would need to be replaced soon, but the shutters had already been done and from the window seat on the landing she could look over the garden through a frame of roses. Things came in packages, he had said. If she wanted to be free from the pressures of maintaining the house she would have to be free from the house. All of the house. And there was no other house like this one in the world.

She thought of the new flats with a shudder: identical boxes, easy to look after, harder to love. And she imagined life without Andrew, who was far from perfect, but was the only man for her and who was also a package deal. What had she been thinking?

Wherever she went, whoever she was with, there would always be things that needed fixing. This house was her home. Andrew was her husband. If they were worth having they were worth the effort. And she couldn't bear to think of leaving either one. There would be some talking to do, some apologising, but she could cope with that.

Sarah phoned the estate agent and told him that she had reconsidered, then she picked up a large piece of paper. She needed to make a new list.

Hive Talking

by Leigh Forbes

Gerald puffed a little more smoke into the hive and watched the bees scurry down between the frames of wax. Carefully, he lifted one frame out and inspected it. It was spotlessly clean, like new. Bees were so uncomplaining, he thought. He'd taken all their honey, and still they cleaned his equipment for him. He murmured his thanks, and stacked the frame with others beside the hive, where they waited to go into winter storage.

The bees must have sensed his happy anticipation, he decided, because they had worked especially hard for him this year, producing an extra twenty jars of honey per hive. An extra twenty jars each equalled... he grinned as he worked it out... three hundred pounds more for the honeymoon fund.

Sunshine and relaxation, he thought, here we come.

'I need a second honeymoon,' Deirdre had complained four years previously. 'We haven't been anywhere even half decent since we were married.'

Gerald remembered sighing a little at this remark, aware that Deirdre's idea of half-decent was the same as everyone else's idea of luxury. He was rather fond of Cornwall, where they'd never been, so he'd suggested that.

'Why can't you take me abroad for once,' she said, before reciting all her friends' exotic holiday-destinations for that year.

When he could finally get a word in, he said, 'Where would you like to go?'

'Well, I've always wanted to go to Singapore and stay in that Raffles Hotel. I really fancy sitting on the balcony sipping a pink gin.' She cackled derisively, before dropping the laugh in favour of a scowl. 'But I suppose a package to Malaga will do. I don't really care, as long as I don't have to stay in a caravan for once. It's got to be a fortnight mind. And at least four stars.' She gestured at the expensive styling of their living room. 'I've kept house all these years, Gerald, and made a wonderful home for you to live in.' She leaned back in her chair and folded her arms. 'I deserve it.'

Gerald wondered if he deserved it too, given the 60-hour weeks he'd put in to pay for it all, but thought it best not to mention that just then. Instead, he slipped quietly away to work out how long it would take to save for a fortnight at Raffles Hotel. He had four years until their silver wedding anniversary; maybe that would be long enough. He was going to need some help, though. His bus driver's salary would never stretch to a luxury foreign holiday, not with Deirdre's love of clothes shopping, and shoe shopping, and handbag shopping, too. But he had lots of friends. Lots. And he knew they would help.

So, later that day, he went to talk to them, just like he did every afternoon. Sitting on the bench beside their hive, he told them all about Singapore, and about Raffles Hotel.

'So, do you think you could do it?' he asked, watching them buzz by, legs heavy with pollen. 'I'll get you some help. You won't have to do it by yourselves.'

He wasn't sure, but he thought he detected a slight rise in the humming, as though sixty-thousand pairs of wings had just started flapping a little harder.

'What are you doing?' Deirdre asked him that evening, as he circled small ads in *Beekeepers' Monthly*.

'I'm going to take you on a second honeymoon.'

'Oh, yeah?' She cast a disdainful glance over the adverts for second-hand hive-tools and smokers. 'Doesn't look like a travel brochure to me.'

'Well, trips to Malaga don't come cheap.'

'Malaga?' A flicker of interest caught in her voice. 'What are you going to do? Sell your bee stuff? At last?'

'No,' he replied. 'I'm going to get more hives, breed more bees, and make more honey. If I can sell twelve jars a week, I'll have enough to take you away for our twenty-fifth.'

Deirdre's mouth worked soundlessly for a moment.

'*More* bees?' she finally spluttered. 'Don't you think you have enough already?'

Gerald so wanted to tell her about Singapore – he'd have loved nothing more than to make his wife happy at last – but he knew he had to keep it a secret, just in case he couldn't pull it off.

'I'm doing my best, love,' he said quietly. 'Just you wait and see.'

'I'm not waiting *four years* for a poxy trip to Malaga,' she said, and stormed out of the room.

For the first time in his marriage, Gerald felt a creeping uncertainty. Deirdre didn't like honey. She was always complaining about the time he spent looking after the hive, and she certainly didn't care about the bees themselves. He wondered if it were fair to ask them to pay for her holiday, especially when she would never thank them for it. She probably wouldn't even thank him for it. But she was his wife, and she had made a nice home, just like she said. She deserved a nice holiday. And, he'd decided he deserved a nice holiday too.

After two years of hard work, Gerald and the bees had managed to save half the amount needed for a week at Raffles Hotel. Deirdre complained loudly the whole time.

'It's just an excuse to muck about in the garden wearing fancy dress,' she said spitefully. 'If you weren't such a nerd, Gerald, I'd be worried about you.'

He had tried hinting that if she spent a bit less money on other things, they could save more quickly for the holiday, but this had been met with a withering stare, and the suggestion he get a better job.

Gerald apologised to the bees for his wife's lack of faith. He explained that once he surprised her with the truth about Singapore, she'd come round.

The bees' buzzing encouraged him to think positively. Good things come to those who wait, they seemed to be saying, as they turned back to their work. For two more years they worked, without complaining.

Gerald finished stacking the frames, and closed up the hive. The bees had been right; something good had come at the end of all the waiting. He thanked them again, and breathed a word of thanks to Deirdre, too. If she hadn't run off with that cruise-ticket-waving bloke from the social club, he'd have never joined the beekeepers' club and met Sally. And if he'd never met Sally, he'd have never known how nice it was to spend time with a woman who liked honey, was interested in bees, and who had been happy to wait for a decent holiday.

Gerald smiled at the hives, thinking what a riot the bees would cause if they accompanied the pair of them tomorrow. It was a bit unfair that they couldn't come – after all, they had paid for the whole shebang: the champagne, the cake, the dress, the church and, of course, the honeymoon in Cornwall.

A Day To Remember

by Helen Kara

I'm lying in bed, listening to Kate clatter in the kitchen, salivating at the smell of bacon, and wondering whether it's time to stop living a lie. Then I think it's not a lie for me, and my mind goes round in the old circle, as familiar as the roundabout at the top of our road. The next exit is signposted Ross. Like me, he would have been fifty this year. What would he think of the mess Kate and I have made of our lives? I don't try to work that out this time, I just keep circling round and round in my head like a driver with a broken satnav.

'Mike! Breakfast!'

I jump out of bed and have a quick look at myself in the mirror. Still in good shape. Maybe it's not too late to find someone who loves me. But I wouldn't love someone else, because I love Kate. Even now my heart lifts at the thought of seeing her.

She is sitting at the table with her bowl of cereal and I give her a friendly kiss on the cheek. There's a plate for me with scrambled eggs, bacon, mushrooms and toast.

'Looks grand. Thank you.'

I tuck in happily, all my cares forgotten. Then Kate says, 'It's a nice day.'

She's right, so I nod.

'I think the bluebells will be out.'

I've just put a forkful of food in my mouth, so I don't need to answer straight away, which is lucky because I want to swear. I should have seen this coming. She has to go to the bluebell wood every year, like a pilgrimage, which is daft because neither of us is a pilgrim.

'I don't think about Ross every day any more,' I say. 'Do you?'

It came out a bit sharp. Her head goes down and my heart contracts. She answers so quietly that I only just catch her word.

'No.'

'Shall we take a picnic?' I ask. 'Make a day of it?'

This has the desired result; she lifts her head and gives me a smile that reaches the soft sides of her eyes.

'Let's do that,' she says.

So I hop into the shower, and check the oil and water levels in the car before we leave, keeping Kate safe like I always promised Ross. I don't do it for him, though. Haven't done for years. I do it for me.

Kate knows I've loved her since the moment we met. I'd been looking forward to meeting her, because Ross was so lit up about his new girlfriend, and Ross, well, we'd known each other since infant school and what made him happy made me happy. I wasn't prepared for the shock of seeing her big brown eyes in her little pale face and wanting to protect her and make her laugh and tell her all the thoughts in my head. Of course, I didn't say anything. When I was best man at their wedding, it was odd really, half my heart was singing in church for the happiness of two people I loved so much, and half was wailing lonely in the wilderness. There was some sadness, too, because the wedding was so rushed and they only had three days' honeymoon in Bournemouth before Ross and I sailed for the Falklands.

We thought the long wait on the boat would be the worst part, innocent boys that we were. Ross said several times that if anything happened to him, I must look after Kate. I always said don't be daft, nothing's going to happen to you, we'll look out for each other and come home together when the war is over. I regretted that, after. Then we got to the action and realised the journey hadn't been the worst part. When Ross took a bullet, a few yards from me, I knew at once he was a goner. I did everything I could to save him, but he died instantly. At least I had that comfort to give to Kate.

I couldn't help her, though, over Anna. She'd written to tell Ross she was pregnant the day before the officers came to break the news of his death. They asked if there was anyone they could call to sit with her, but she said no, she wanted to be alone for a while. Then she drove to the bluebell wood, which had been a special place for her and Ross, and spent some time among all that beauty trying to balance sorrow and joy and come to terms with tragedy.

When Kate's daughter was born that autumn she was so happy. I was home by then, and delighted the baby was a girl, because I thought she would never have to know the horrors of war. Another mistake. Anna's just like her dad, and was determined to follow in his footsteps. She's a Corporal now, in Afghanistan.

I told Kate I loved her before Anna was born. She was kind, even appreciative, but Ross was the only man she'd ever loved. I was glad to be able to talk to her about him and I think she felt the same. I told her I would settle for friendship, and offered her and the baby my protection and support. After Anna was born, as Kate had no family nearby, I ended up staying in her house. Soon Anna began calling me "Daddy". We explained to her about Ross, and showed her the photos, but as far as she was concerned I was her daddy and "Daddy Ross" was a man in a picture. The wedding photos were her favourite, with Mummy in a "princess dress".

I'll never forget the day she came running in from pre-school with a picture she'd drawn.

'Look, Daddy. Look, Mummy.' She put the picture on the coffee table. 'I've done a picture of your wedding. Mummy, you're wearing your princess dress again. And, look, I would be a bridesmaid and wear my own princess dress.' Anna grinned at us with the complacent look of someone who has solved a problem, and scampered off to watch TV.

Kate backed away from me and stood against the sink. 'I guess it would be better for Anna if we were married.'

'It might be better for us,' I said hopefully.

'I know how you feel.' She folded her arms. 'And you know how I feel. If you're still willing to get married, and have a low-key wedding...'

'You would marry me?'

She nodded.

'Why, when you don't love me?'

'I'm fond of you. You're a kind man. You were Ross's friend, and you're a great dad to Anna. It's a good deal for me because I'm never going to love anyone like I love Ross. I'm not sure it's such a good deal for you.'

It's taken me twenty-odd years, but I think Kate had a point. I was daft, really. I thought she would change, that I could change her, if I loved her enough. I suppose I should talk to her about this, work out what to do. I don't want to hurt her, but I need my life back.

It'll have to wait, though, because we've reached the bluebell wood. I park up and fetch the cool box from the boot. We walk into the wood and it is glorious, ribbons of sunlight slanting through the bright green leaves, the ground carpeted in luminous blue. A path runs down towards the stream and there are picnic tables set among the flowers.

I put the cool box on one of the tables. Kate looks a bit jittery. She doesn't meet my eyes.

'Mike, can we walk down to the stream?'

I take her hand. 'Of course.'

Ross's ashes were scattered in that stream on the first anniversary of his death. I put my arm around Kate's shoulders and we stare at the water rushing and bubbling over its stony bed. It's a soothing sight and it takes me a while to spot that she is crying quietly. I hold her closer and tell her it's okay to cry.

She pulls away from me and swipes the tears from her cheeks. 'No it's not. It's not okay at all.'

I trot out those wise words from her bereavement counsellor. 'Grief has no sell-by date.'

'Grief has nothing to do with it. I've been so stupid.' She's glaring at me now as if I'm in trouble. 'About you and me. I should never have let it go on this long.'

So she's giving me the old heave-ho. Not much of a surprise, really.

'I'm so sorry, Mike,' she says. 'I've been really unfair to

you. I—' She stops, swallows, looks determined. 'I love you.'

Starburst fireworks explode in my chest and I wonder whether I'm going to pass out. My head is swimming, but I can hear the splashy sounds of the stream, smell the grassy scent of the bluebells, and feel the longed-for touch of Kate's beloved lips on mine. Her arms go around me, anchoring me to the earth, and I open my eyes to see the beautiful face of my wife with love in her eyes, for me, at last.

Performing by Proxy

by Jenny Maltby

Fred Fowle pulled the collar of his long black coat up while casting his pale blue eyes down to the ground as if in prayer. He didn't usually look after the funerals of people he knew; he found it easier when there was some emotional distance between the grieving and, of course, there was always the fact that it just seemed plain wrong to make money from his acquaintances' deaths. On this occasion, however, he had been persuaded by Bea McQueen to make an exception and, as always, she had got what she wanted. The funeral had to be "a little bit different, Freddie darling, something special to reflect who Brian was". Special Brian's wife had had no say in the matter.

Fred Fowle sighed as he watched them gather under the bullet grey sky. Not an ounce of dignity between them. Even at Brian's funeral, they were dressed like peacocks, none of them wanting to be outdone. None of them wanting to go into the church to sit with Brian's wife who gazed into space alone. As always, they were waiting for the drama. Fred was caught between the overexcited chattering outside and the music inside the church. Not the usual piped organ, but a soundtrack of Gilbert and Sullivan overtures, determinedly romping and utterly, utterly unsuitable for a funeral.

They swept past him now, a clump of chattering colour. No black clothes at this funeral, Bea McQueen had declared. Brian would not approve. Sadly, no one had bothered to mention this fact to the grieving widow who now blended into the church corner, not part of the main cast. She had no role to play, but seemed quietly resigned to this fact. Fred Fowle knew just how she felt. Bea McQueen glided regally into the front pew, a large netted hat covering all but her vermillion lips, the waft of her trademark Youth Dew re-igniting the space in his mind that was still simmering with memories of her cloyingly close proximity just weeks earlier.

The memory was still sharp as a newly-carved headstone. Fred had never stood so still before, unable even to breathe. Bea McQueen had towered over him, waiting for him to perform. He saw himself as others saw him: terrified and out of his depth as she wound her way slowly around him, fingers trailing teasingly across his clenched cheek. Her hands were colder than they had been in his daydreams. The music swelled around him as he braced himself for her calculated seduction.

Just as she was about to declare her undying love, there was a big commotion and the music petered out. Typical.

Bea's face broke into a huge smile and she flicked her tongue lightly over her teeth. They were slightly too white, Fred noticed, glistening and pointy. She was like the big, bad wolf; she'd eat him alive and not even spit out the bones.

'*Dah*-ling, I *knew* you wouldn't let me down,' Bea screeched to the back of the hall.

‘Sorry I’m late. Sorry everyone. Sorry,’ came the deep tones of Brian.

Brian didn’t sound sorry at all. Not as sorry as Fred was, at any rate. Bloody Brian with his bluster and baritone voice. Fred Fowle had waited his turn for years to be seduced by Bea McQueen, trying not to mind as all the other men buzzed and swarmed around her, hoping to become her leading man.

Fred left the stage unnoticed. He’d never be the lead, especially with the likes of Baritone Brian to compete with. He could carry a tune of course – it was, apparently, his lack of stage presence that discounted him from even reaching the final auditions. Where did the others dig it out from? Even Geoff Taylor, the nondescript lending manager of the small local branch of Barclays, managed to morph into someone else once he got on stage, strutting about in ridiculous outfits and fussing about his make-up.

Fred didn’t fit into this menagerie of outlandish and extravagant figures. He was used to blending into the shadows – in fact, he’d made a career of it: Fred Fowle, the funeral assistant.

Granny’s funeral had been his epiphany. There had been much debate as to whether a funeral was really the place for a 9-year-old boy, his tight-lipped parents finally deciding that it was “better to learn about life”; and along he’d gone, uncomplainingly. He’d watched wide-eyed as everyone seemed to float in, enveloped in black from top to bottom, snuffling into perfectly white handkerchiefs without actually making a fuss. It wasn’t as good as going to the cinema or anything, but there was something about it that struck a chord in him. He couldn’t put it into words, the way he felt, the way he could sense everyone’s thoughts about each other. But then it happened. As Uncle Bob stood up in the pulpit to give his run-down on Granny's few redeeming features, the sun had sneaked from behind the huge rolls of cloud hanging over the church, burst through the stained glass windows and enveloped Uncle Bob in rainbow prisms. Fred had glanced around. He wasn't sure whether anyone else had noticed and, if they had, wondered whether they thought it was a message from God, too. He did things like that, God, miracles and stuff. But whatever it was, oh! The indoor rainbow and the wrong notes on the organ combined to ignite a love of funerals that had made him what he was today.

Fred wound his way from the tatty backstage area to the auditorium, letting the lumpy velvet seat accommodate his weary body. Bea was now winding herself around Brian and the orchestra piping up again with melodious encouragement, the violin bows bobbing up and down in unison. Fred loved the way an orchestra sounded, but there was something about the way it looked too, the metronomic regularity of it, the reassuring glances between players and conductor. They seemed connected somehow, symbiotically held together by theme and rhythm. Perhaps he should have played an instrument – musicians always seemed a good bunch, less competitive and happy enough to be shrouded in black and stuck in a pit. Fred considered that this might have done him very nicely. Perhaps if he learned about music, he could write a new soundtrack for his life. Reinvent himself. As it stood, the overture to his life would definitely be written in a melancholy key. A Minor, no doubt. If only he were a B Major, things would surely be different.

Perhaps it was too late to be someone else. When he was fifteen, a new boy had joined the school, much to the excitement of the girls. The boy bristled with anger and had, apparently, been expelled from the private boys' school for setting fire to palm trees. Fred Fowle had avoided him, not because he was scared, particularly, but because even standing close to someone like that would show Fred up for the plain wallpaper he was destined to become. At least now he didn't stand out as boring – he merely became invisible. Was that better or worse? It was certainly too late to start setting fire to trees.

The chorus congregated on the stage. Fred Fowle had pushed to be made understudy, but now he rather regretted not being a part of the 'gang'. He would not appear on stage at all unless something terrible happened to Brian. Enforced memory loss, perhaps, for the ultimate in 'corpsing'.

'Leonard Meryll, faced his peril, death in most appalling shape' sang the chorus forcefully.

They were a funny lot, mused Fred. Without the make up and the costumes and lighting, they looked like a total rabble. You wouldn't see any one of them in the street and think that they harboured desires for treading the boards yet here they were, the same group of people year after year, swapping affections and gossip as only the very amateur dramatic could. Of course, in his line of work, Fred had realised many years ago just what hidden depths people could have, even in a small town like this. He knew all sorts of things about people; one of the perks of his job was that the grieving could be very indiscreet. He could write a book about it, but who would believe it was real? In fact, the way they carried on, it was a wonder there weren't more deaths in peculiar circumstances. Fred Fowle's eyes narrowed as he watched Brian sticking his oar into a scene he wasn't involved in.

Fred stood outside the stage door, dragging heavily on his cigarette. He tended to smoke on his own – it made his reluctance to share his packet easier. Not that he was mean, but the enhanced high produced from soaking his fags in embalming fluid wasn't for everyone. He could hear the fuss and rumble inside of a scene change. He liked this stage of rehearsals when everything was all out of order, a random mish-mash of plot and confused voices. His working life was based on the natural order of things. It must be good to play God and mix it up a bit. Put your own stamp on how things were played out. Perhaps they'd let him direct a production sometime. He liked the idea of ordering Baritone Brian's execution. He liked it very much, in fact.

The funeral was an abomination. Worse, in fact. Fred Fowle was ashamed that he had ever got involved. The church was packed and, if bums on seats was what counted, then Baritone Brian – not to mention Bea McQueen – would have been pleased. The whole thing just seemed slightly out of kilter. Of course, Brian's untimely death had been typically dramatic and oh yes! in full costume and make-up if you please. Did the man have no shame? Fred Fowle had to admit, though, dying on-stage mid-dress rehearsal had a certain poetic justice about it. It reminded him of the bizarre disbelief that had been shared when Tommy Cooper had died on-stage. He'd seen that on the television. Live at the Palladium. Something incongruous like that. Poor old Tommy had collapsed and the longer he lay there, the more the titters in the audience grew until the joke had clearly expired, along with the laughs and, ultimately, Tommy. Dying in front of his audience. Fred's sense of irony had been keenly filtered through his love of the macabre. There really weren't enough perfectly ironic deaths in life. Health freaks choking on a single goat hair in their disgusting chalky milk, for example.

Reverend Thomas did the necessary, though Fred couldn't help thinking that even he looked perkier than usual, as if he was auditioning for a cameo role – he looked liked himself, but was he wearing eye liner?

Marion watched them all snuffling into their tissues, making sure that they didn't smudge their make-up or knock the carefully jaunty tilt of their oversized hats. These past few weeks had been, well, strange. Brian dying like that, all of a sudden – well, she hadn't expected that. She was, of course, used to being on her own. Sunday afternoons drifted into Sunday evenings as the rehearsals turned into drinking sessions in places she'd never been invited to, with people she'd never met. Of course, over the years, she had come to know of the various members of the G&S Society. She saw them all fawning over each other, that Bea McQueen always at the centre of any scandal. Bea McQueen indeed. Marion knew that wasn't her real name – as Beatrice Clark, she'd had quite a reputation up north. No wonder she'd moved down here and abandoned her accent. Marion might not have had what it took to infiltrate their merry crew of luvvies, but she knew how to do her research. Oh, yes. She had copies of all the operettas that had been performed over the years; she knew the score, as it were, and she had smiled quietly at Fred Fowle in the library a few weeks ago. She liked quiet, slim, grey Fred – in her humble opinion, they should have given him the role of Jack Point, she thought, seeing how he gazed at Bea. He was the sort to stand on the sidelines, just like her. The music jogged along as her memory filled in the words of the various songs covered in the overture.

'It is sung to the moon by a love-lorn loon, Who fled from the mocking throng, O!'... He had hidden depths, did Fred Fowle, and a perfect name for the stage. He'd been so kind to her over the past few weeks and she felt bad that she'd taken advantage. Bless him that he thought she was really interested in his work. In all honesty, the place had given her the shivers. But she had been doing it for him as much as for herself and he was none the wiser. She had played him in just the same way that Bea McQueen, as Phoebe, had tricked Brian's 'Wilfred', distracting him as she borrowed his keys and took what she needed. 'Were I thy Bride' indeed. Fred was too sensible to fall for that overpainted, heaving bosomed floozy, wasn't he?

Marion hadn't seen the accident, of course. But Fred, lovely kind Fred, had been there, sitting in the shadows of his understudy world, just as Marion herself had done all these years in her marriage to Brian.

It had happened just as Brian had won the scheming Phoebe for his wife. Everyone had expressed their amusement as he'd tottered about dramatically, finally falling into the orchestra pit and cracking his head against the piano. Marion supposed she should feel bad, but it had been an accident. A sprinkling of embalming fluid in his endless cups of decaf coffee would be just the thing to make his throat burn and render him unable to perform. She hadn't paid much heed to the other side-effects and didn't want to draw attention to herself in the library by being spotted looking up the poisoning qualities of Fred Fowle's tools of the trade.

She dabbed at her eyes with the perfectly white handkerchief Fred had thoughtfully handed her and tried to ignore the jangle of keys in his pocket as he patted her arm. An accident, she convinced herself. She was surprised that such a small amount had had such a drastic effect.

Next to her, Fred Fowle was thinking the same thing... he'd only meant to make Brian too ill to perform. It had worked, though, and Fred was the understudy no more.

All around them, dressed in their peacock colours, the chorus' single line of song built from nothing into a swelling crescendo that filled the church... 'Sing us your song now...'

Marion would never be an amateur dramatic widow again. She was practically a professional now.

Never Too Late

by Deborah Carr

I couldn't believe it was almost a year since my mother was widowed and, even though Jack wasn't my father, he was in my life for almost as long as I could remember. I missed him and I knew she did, too. Despite her reassurances, I liked to help her as much as I could. You know what I mean, things like the weekly shopping, although she insisted it wasn't necessary, especially as she was buying about a third of the amount of food she used to.

I sent my husband Dave around every so often, too, to make sure she didn't need any light bulbs changing, heavy boxes lifting and so on. I couldn't imagine how I'd cope without Dave doing all the usual jobs men seem so keen to carry out: mowing, for example. Especially now that my mother seemed to be a little more distant every time I spoke to her, I knew she needed these things to be taken care of.

Jack had always been the one in charge of running the house. He believed it was the man's job and hated Mum doing anything like climbing ladders or endangering herself in any way. After all, she had two children to bring up and was needed elsewhere in the home.

'It must be so lonely for her now,' I said to Dave when he

returned home, having popped in to Mum's on the way back from work.

'She seems fine to me,' he said, dunking a digestive into his sugary tea and groaning as half of it disintegrated into the hot fluid. 'I think you worry too much, Sue.'

I wrung out the dishcloth and draped it over the taps.

'How can you say that? Haven't you noticed how she's been losing weight these past few months?' I asked, wondering why I was the only one to see how much support she needed. 'If we don't help her out, then who will? It's not as if my brother is going to. Too busy enjoying himself with trips around the world.'

Dave shook his head and smiled at me. 'Sue, he's a pilot. He's working and travelling – it's what pilots do. Anyway, your mum really does seem fine to me.'

What would he know? I wondered. His mother still had her husband with her. They were always going out to lunch and visiting local craft exhibitions. They had more than enough in their lives. What did poor Mum have to keep her busy now?

'Did you fix the handle on the kitchen cupboard door for her, like I asked you to?' I asked to his back as he left the room.

Dave nodded. 'Of course.'

At least I could cross that job off my list of Things To Do. I dried my hands and went out into the hall and called Mum. The phone rang for longer than her usual five or six rings and I started to feel the old familiar panic rising in my chest.

'Hello, darling,' she said, her voice a little weary.

'How did you know it was me?' I asked, trying to remember not to frown. I didn't need to worry about wrinkles as well as everything else.

'It's five-thirty. You usually call about this time.'

I wondered briefly whether she was irritated with me, before dismissing the idea. 'I'm cooking us a roast chicken tonight and wanted to ask you if you'd like me to make you up a plate. Dave can drop it round to you when it's ready.'

'That's a lovely thought, Sue, thank you,' she said, 'but I should think Dave would like to sit down for a bit now that he's home, so please don't worry about me.'

'He won't mind, Mum, and at least I'll know you've eaten a proper meal.'

'Honestly, there's no need to bother,' she said, her voice a little softer. 'I've already eaten enough today.'

'When?' I asked. She only ever bothered with a sandwich or a can of soup at lunchtimes and rarely seemed to cook Jack's favourite 'meat and two veg' type meals now she didn't have to.

'Oh, didn't I say?'

'What, Mum?' I could feel that frown reappearing once again on my forehead.

'Janice and Sophie, the sisters who recently moved in down the road from me, invited me to join them for their weekly splash out meal at the Italian restaurant nearby.'

I tried to recollect the women and seemed to recall two bubble-permed blondes with rather excitable voices from the last time I popped in to Mum's house with some shopping for her. 'That's kind of them. Did you have a nice time?'

'Lovely, thank you. Now why don't you get along and put your feet up this evening? I promise I'm fine and dandy and you truly don't need to worry about me.'

'Well, all right then,' I said. 'I'll see you tomorrow at ten-thirty.'

'What for?'

Her question only confirmed my concern about her diminishing memory. She never seemed to recall much of what I told her since Jack had died.

'Mum, remember I was going to give you a lift to the doctor's for your check-up.'

She groaned. 'I'd forgotten about that. You really don't need to, Sue, I'm more than happy to catch the bus. The stop is just down the road.'

'Don't be silly,' I laughed. 'It's no trouble at all. I'll see you then.'

The following morning Dave finished his breakfast and gave me a peck on the cheek. 'Bye love. Have a good day.'

I smiled as he closed the front door behind him, thanking my lucky stars for the millionth time that I'd listened to my stepfather and married such a solid, dependable man. I could rely on him for anything. I lifted my cup of tea to my lips and was just about to take a sip when the door opened and Dave strode in.

'What's the matter?' I asked.

He shrugged. 'Just going to change your tyre, I noticed you've got a flat.'

'Thanks,' I said, realising I had to phone Mum to let her know I'd be a little late getting to her house.

I dialled her number and let the phone ring.

'Something's happened,' I called out to Dave.

When I didn't receive a reply I ran out to him. 'Dave, I just know Mum's had an accident.'

'Why do you think that?' he asked over his shoulder as he loosened the bolts on the wheel.

I felt sick. 'She's not answering her phone.'

'Bathroom, maybe? Give her a few minutes and try again. If there's no answer then, I'll call in on my way to work, but I'm sure she'll be fine. Stop getting in such a state about her. You're turning into your stepdad.'

I paced the hall and then retried her number. As it rang, I thought over Dave's snapped comment. What was wrong with being like Jack? He was a lovely man, always organised and caring.

'Dave, please go and check on her. She's still not answering.'

He finished changing the tyre and after washing his hands took me by the shoulders. 'Stop worrying. I'm going right now,' he soothed. 'I'll call you from my mobile as soon as I get there.'

The five minute journey seemed to take forever. *Where was he?* I wondered, as I stared at the silent phone willing it to ring, nearly jumping when it finally did. 'Yes? Is everything okay?'

'Hello, darling,' said Mum sounding, I thought, a little guilty. 'Dave said I have to let you know I'm fine and that I haven't had an accident or anything.'

Relief coursed though me. 'Thank heavens for that.'

'Tell her where you were,' I heard Dave say in the background, seeming rather amused.

'Mum? What is he talking about? Where were you?'

Mum sighed. 'At the gym,' she said, her voice almost a whisper.

'Sorry, I thought you said you'd been at the gym.'

There was a pause, before Dave encouraged her to continue.

'I was, darling. I've been going to the gym early in the morning three times a week for the past six months. Haven't you noticed how much weight I've lost?'

I couldn't take it in. The entire time I'd been worried about her losing weight, believing it to be grief, she'd been working out at the gym.

'Isn't that a little dangerous at your age?' I couldn't help asking.

'Sue, I'm seventy, not a hundred and ten. I take it very easy. I'm feeling healthier than I have in years and am finally losing the weight I've carried for so long.'

'But there was nothing wrong with you before. Jack always said so.'

'I loved your stepdad, Sue, but if I ever wanted to do anything different or change myself in any way he always fussed and refused to let me. Much as I miss him, and I do, I'm also enjoying having time to myself to do the things I've always wanted to do without having to get approval from someone else first.'

'Me, you mean?' It was starting to dawn on me how much I'd been suffocating her this past year.

Mum laughed. 'Yes, you. I know you're only looking out for me, but I've been trying to find a way to tell you that you don't need to worry quite so much. I'm more than capable of looking after myself and for the first time in my adult life I have the freedom to do so.'

I'd never heard my mother seem so independent before. 'I worry about you, that's all.'

'I know, dear, but maybe you should concentrate a little more on your own marriage. You have a good man there, you know.'

She was right. Dave could never do enough for me or my family and only ever wanted to make me happy. Perhaps it was time I focused a little bit more on him rather than worrying unnecessarily about Mum.

'Will you be catching the bus to the doctor's today, then?' I asked, just to make sure she didn't need me.

'No, I've cancelled the appointment. He only wanted to check on me because he's been a family friend for so long. There's nothing wrong with me, darling. I'm fine.'

And for the first time since Jack had died I could tell that for myself.

'I know, Mum. Have a good day. I'll see you soon.'

As I put down the phone I noticed the flyer Dave had placed on the worktop the day before, advertising a new Italian restaurant.

Smiling, I picked up the phone again and began dialling.

Dinner in Paradise

by Cally Taylor

I'd had the framed photo for as long as I could remember. It had moved with me from my childhood bedroom, to my university digs and then, finally, to my own home where I hung it on the dining room wall before I did anything else. Simon thought it was silly, but I loved the way the man and woman looked so happy together, his arm round her waist, her head on his shoulder as they stared out to a sunset sea, a sumptuous meal on a candlelit table beside them.

I'd spotted the photo at a car boot sale when I was eleven, and was immediately drawn to its paradise setting and romantic image. In my mind the man had just proposed to the woman and she'd said yes.

My recently divorced mother smiled ruefully when I asked for fifty pence so I could buy it.

'Wouldn't you rather have the My Little Pony picture?' she asked, gesturing further up the table.

'No, thank you,' I said, hugging my find to my chest. 'I want this one. When I grow up my life's going to be just like this photo.'

'Good luck with that,' my mother said, reluctantly snapping open her purse.

I spent years staring at that photo, dreaming that one day I'd find a man who'd whisk me away to paradise, arrange a romantic meal on the sandy shore and prove my cynical mother wrong.

'Alison,' Simon called from the house. 'Dinner's ready.'

I put down my soldering iron and smiled. What would it be tonight? Eggs and chips? Jacket potato and beans? Sausages and mash? It was great that my boyfriend took his turn at making the dinner, especially as I'd spent all of Saturday making jewellery in my shed-cum-workshop, but he was physically incapable of making anything that didn't involve potatoes.

'How's it going?' he asked as he placed a plate of crispy fish fingers and singed chips in front of me. 'Did you finish that order?'

'Nearly,' I said, reaching for the ketchup and squirting a large dollop on the edge of the plate. 'If I put in another hour after dinner I think I'll be done.'

Simon gazed at me from across the table, his plate of food untouched.

'What?' I said, a forkful of breaded fish touching my lips.

'*Another* hour?' he said.

'Well yes,' I said. 'It's a customised silver bracelet. I have to engrave some daisies on it.'

Simon let out a long, exasperated sigh. 'You're always in that blimmin shed, Ali. I thought we were supposed to be having a clear-out for the charity shop and then going out. We never spend any time together anymore.'

'I'm sorry,' I said guiltily, my eyes flicking up to my adored photo on the wall behind him. 'Really I am, but would you mind doing the charity stuff before your shift on Monday? We'll go out soon, I promise. I'll be cutting down the amount of time I spend making jewellery. Honestly.'

It was true. After Sunday jewellery-making could become an enjoyable hobby again instead of a crazed money-making scheme. All I had to do was sell a hundred pounds' worth of stock at the craft fair and I'd have enough saved for a very, very special holiday to Mauritius for the two of us.

Simon and I had been together for five years, but we were no closer to getting engaged than the first day we'd met. It wasn't that he didn't want to marry me; he frequently told me how much he loved me and wanted to spend the rest of his life with me, but there was no way he'd be able to afford my paradise dream in a million years, no matter how hard he worked as a nurse at our local hospital. I had a good job as a Sales Executive at a computer software company, but I needed the extra from my jewellery business to put into my 'paradise dream' savings account (stuffed in an old handbag and tucked behind a pile of old clothes in the bedroom wardrobe). With the money well hidden instead of in our bank account Simon wouldn't get suspicious and spoil my surprise.

Mum was horrified when I told her I was going to propose.

'You can't do that, Alison,' she'd squawked down the phone when I broke the news in hushed tones one evening while Simon was 'cooking' sausages and chips.

'Why not?' I'd replied.

'I never realised you were such a feminist,' she'd said. 'When you were little I don't remember you telling me you thought it was Cinderella who should try and cram a size ten loafer on Prince Charming's foot.'

'That's because I was a child,' I said defensively. 'Anyway, it doesn't matter who does the asking, just as long as the answer's yes.'

'If that's what you believe then good on you,' Mum said. 'But if Simon was any kind of a man he'd do the proposing.'

I was so annoyed I nearly slammed the phone down on her. Instead, I took a deep breath and changed the subject. It wasn't just the slur on Simon's manliness that hurt; she'd touched a nerve. I know it sounds a bit old-fashioned, but I'd always imagined that the man I was going to spend the rest of my life with would get down on one knee. But a dream was a dream and I wasn't going to get my romantic sunset meal unless I took matters into my own, slightly blistered, hands.

'How did it go?' Simon asked wearily when I returned from the craft fair and wandered into the living room, my 'savings handbag' hidden behind my back.

'Not great,' I lied, hiding my glee at selling over two hundred pounds' worth of jewellery behind a fake frown. 'I only sold a couple of pairs of earrings.'

'That was worth it then,' he said, looking back at the TV. 'Brilliant.'

It broke my heart to see him so annoyed. That morning, after he'd surprised me with breakfast in bed, he'd suggested we go for a walk along Southend seafront, have an ice cream on the pier and play the penny arcade. I'd said no, apologetically, and reminded him about the craft fair. The look on his face said it all. I'd let him down again, putting my hobby before quality time together.

'I'll just put my stuff away,' I said, heading off to the bedroom with my bag, 'and then we'll snuggle up on the sofa and watch a film together.'

He didn't reply.

The next day I hurried back from work, checked Simon had already left for his night shift at the hospital, and scurried into the bedroom. My plan was to transfer all the jewellery takings from my secret handbag into my work bag and visit the travel agent's during my lunch break the next day.

I threw open the wardrobe door and my breath caught in my throat.

It was empty. The bag was gone.

'No!' I shouted, running from room to room, lifting cushion covers, opening cupboards, peering under beds and pulling back sofa. '*No!*'

I returned to the bedroom and stared at the empty wardrobe. The bag had definitely gone. How could I have been so stupid? I fished my mobile out of my pocket with trembling fingers and stabbed at the buttons.

'Simon,' I said as soon as I heard his hushed hello, 'please tell me you didn't take all the bags in the wardrobe to the charity shop.'

'Alison I'm at work,' he whispered. 'You know I can't talk at—'

'But it's really, really important. Did you go to the charity shop today?'

'Of course I did,' he said. 'You asked me to on Saturday.'

'But... but...' I stuttered, the words catching in my throat.

'What's the matter? Did I forget to take something? I took some of my jumpers and a bag of old clothes I found in the wardrobe.'

'My bag,' I said. 'It's gone.'

There was a pause.

'Do you mean the tatty one that was in the back of the

wardrobe?' Simon said finally. 'I didn't give that to the charity shop.'

'Oh thank God,' I breathed, glancing around the room. 'Where is it?'

'On the dump I should think,' he said. 'I threw it away. No one in their right mind would part with good cash for that tatty old thing.'

Something inside me crumpled and my eyes filled with tears. All those months of slaving away in the shed, all that money and a lifetime's dream. Gone.

'Alison?' Simon said. 'Alison are you okay?'

'I'm fine,' I said, swallowing hard.

'Are you sure?'

'I'm sure,' I said.' Look, I'd better go. I love you.'

'I love you too,' he replied, sounding confused.

I hardly slept that night. I even got out of bed at midnight and drove halfway to the dump in my pyjamas and slippers before coming to my senses and turning back. I couldn't tell Simon what had happened. I just couldn't, he'd be too upset. And it wasn't his fault. It was mine.

Alison Brown you are a total idiot, I thought, as I stared at the photograph in the dining room. Love isn't about paradise settings and sea shore meals. It's about being with the man you love, and who loves you more than anyone else in the world. You should be grateful for what you've got, not dreaming foolish dreams.

When I returned home from work on Tuesday, totally exhausted from lack of sleep, I automatically headed for the shed at the back of the garden.

'Alison,' Simon called from the kitchen, 'could you come here for a second?'

'I can't,' I shouted back. 'I need to work on my jewell—'

I stared at the shed door and shook my head. No I didn't. Not anymore.

'Coming,' I called, hurrying down the path and into the kitchen. 'What's up?'

'I thought we'd go out,' he said, reaching for my hand, 'seeing as you're not working tonight.'

'That would be lovely.' I smiled up at him. 'King's Arms for chicken kievs and chips?'

He shook his head. 'Not tonight.'

I had to laugh as Simon sauntered along the pier towards me, two bags of chips in one hand. For one silly second, as we'd wandered down the high street arm in arm, I'd wondered if he'd secretly booked us a table at the fancy French restaurant that had just opened. But no, my potato-loving boyfriend had reverted to type.

'Thank you,' I said, holding out my hands for my chips as he drew closer.

He wrapped an arm around my waist. 'Not yet.'

'What's going on?' I asked, frowning up at him.

'You'll find out,' he said, pulling me closer. 'Come with me.'

I didn't know whether to laugh or cry. There, right at the end of the pier, was a small wooden table, covered with a white table cloth, and two chairs.

'Simon?' I said, turning to look at him, but he'd disappeared.

'Down here,' he said.

And there he was, crouched beside me, on one knee.

'Alison,' he said, gently taking hold of my left hand. 'You are the most infuriating woman in the world. I've been trying to set this up for weeks now, but every time I tried to get you out of the house you insisted on going down to the shed instead.'

'About that,' I said. 'I...'

'Sssh,' Simon held a finger to his mouth and I nodded mutely. 'Alison Brown,' he continued, reaching into his jacket pocket and pulling out a small black box. 'Would you do me the honour of becoming my wife?'

I looked from him, to the steaming chip papers on the table, to the foggy British sunset in the distance and back again. It was perfect. And so was he.

'Yes,' I said, crouching down and throwing my arms around him. 'Oh yes, yes, yes!'

Monkey Business

by Sarah Dunnakey

'Get me a monkey.'

'A monkey?'

'Yes, you know, one of those chimp things. Tea parties, flat caps, funny faces. It's what this show needs.'

Zoe doubted that very much. And they're apes not monkeys she thought, but didn't say. And this isn't a show, it's a village fête. But she didn't say that either.

Ever since Gordon became chair of the Brascombe Village Fête Committee – replacing Ursula who had run the whole thing for the last ten years, but had a funny turn in April and was spending the summer in Ibiza – ever since he took the reins, the event had become more and more like a circus. Literally.

Gordon knew people. Knew people who knew people. And clowns. And animals.

So far he had signed up Charlie Chuckles and his Amazing Bounce-O-Matic Car, a pair of juggling twins and a herd of llamas.

'Do they dance?' Zoe had heard him asking the llama lady over the phone. 'Ah well, never mind. I'm sure we can find a niche for them.'

On Gordon's map of the Event Site – known as Brascombe Primary School field to everyone else – everyone had their niche. The one allocated to the llamas was in the top right hand corner, in-between the bottle pull and the fireman's lifts (real firemen, well a couple of retired ones anyway).

Next to the map was the Order of Events, starting with the Mayoral cutting of the ribbon and culminating in the Crowning of the Brascombe Beauty. The local press often missed the first, but never the last. A pretty girl was always good news for a local paper, but the real draw was the crown itself. Donated fifty years ago by the Dowager Lady Brascombe, the solid silver tiara, encrusted with jewels, always raised a gasp and sparked a frenzy of photograph taking when it was lifted from its box and placed on the Beauty's head.

As Fête Secretary, Treasurer and general Girl Friday, the security of the crown was one of Zoe's many responsibilities, but that was a doddle, she decided, compared to finding a chimpanzee.

'So that monkey, Zoe. Any luck?' Gordon asked on the Tuesday before the fête.

She shook her head and sucked the end of her pen. She had tried everything. The keeper at the local zoo had listened politely to her request and then given her a long lecture on the dangers and general moral badness of using animals as sideshow gimmicks. She took that as a no. She tried various animal sanctuaries and was offered a giant toothless rabbit, a chinchilla with a sock fetish and an axolotl. She almost said yes to the axolotl, even though she wasn't really sure what one was.

'Vicious brutes,' the sanctuary owner said. 'But beautiful,' he added with a sigh.

Zoe declined.

With less than a week to go to the fête, things weren't looking good. One of the juggling twins sprained her wrist, the llamas were through to the final auditions of Animals Have Got Talent and their owner was negotiating for a higher fee, and Mr Chuckles' Bounce-O-Matic car failed its MOT.

'We need that monkey,' said Gordon. His Event Site map was looking bleak. The WI 'Guess the Weight of the Chair' and the Brownies' bric-a-brac were all that was holding it together.

Zoe had tried everything. No, wait. Not everything. She was online, checking the prices of builder's sand to try to solve the problem of the boggy ground at the entrance to the playing field. She typed 'Chimpanzee' and 'Brascombe' into her search engine.

And there he was. Or rather, there they were. Man and chimp.

It was a brief item in the online version of the local newspaper. There was a feature on a pub in the next village. It apparently counted amongst its regulars a man and his chimpanzee. Beauty and the beast, Zoe thought looking at the accompanying photograph. The man had dark curls and a big grin. The chimp in contrast looked quite surly, his eyes beady under the edge of a beanie hat. Zoe thought about what the zoo keeper had said about using animals as gimmicks. Then she glanced over to Gordon's sorry map. Saturday was going to be a long and embarrassing drag. Maybe Gordon was right. Maybe a chimp was just what was needed.

She rang the pub immediately. The landlord seemed to consider her request for a long time and then said, 'Oh yes, I'll let them know.'

'It's for Saturday.'

'Oh, yes.'

'So it's quite urgent.'

'Yes, indeed.'

By five o'clock on Friday afternoon Zoe had given up. The fête would just have to be less than thrilling this year, which when she thought about it was what it had been every year so far. She was about to head home when the phone rang.

'Hi, it's Ralph.'

She didn't know any Ralphs.

'Ralph and Ed.'

'Sorry,' she said 'I...'

'Ralph and Ed, the chimp.'

Of course.

They would be there, he said, would love to be involved, always happy to help out for a good cause. No, no fee, she could buy him a pint sometime, and a coke for Ed.

She'd done it.

Gordon insisted that they celebrate and bought her half a cider and a pickled egg at the Brascombe Arms. He suggested that after Saturday when they both had a bit more free time, maybe she would like to join him for a meal. They did a two for one deal on Thursday. It was a long time since Zoe had had a date, but she managed a polite smile and said no.

The morning of the fête was glorious. A blue sky and a light fresh breeze. The llamas, who were beaten at their TV auditions by a trampolining gerbil, turned up with their heads held high and their 'As seen on Radio Bottershire' banner. The single juggler was already gathering a crowd as she threw flaming torches into the air. And Charlie Chuckles arrived, minus his comedy car, but with a dazzling display of magic that he wove around the swelling crowds. The whole of Brascombe was there. Drawn by the good weather, the smell of freshly baked cakes, and quite possibly the large poster in the Town Square erected by Gordon that morning which declared 'And There Will Be A Chimp'.

And then Ralph and Ed arrived. The star turns. No one was disappointed. Ed sat patiently while he was petted and patted, and every child in the village had their photograph taken with him. Ralph's smile was infectious and added to everyone's enjoyment of the day. Including Zoe, who blushed crimson when Ralph winked at her and told her he was looking forward to that pint she owed him.

By five o'clock Zoe was relaxing in a deckchair with a glass of local cider. Only the Brascombe Beauty crowning to go, then it would all be over for another year. She had handed the crown itself over to the WI Chair who would safeguard it until the ceremony. There was absolutely nothing else for Zoe to do. Gordon sank into the chair next to her.

'My goodness,' he said. 'What a day! I've just collected all the money and you know what, I think we may have doubled last year's takings, in fact...'

He was stopped by a scream.

'Stop! Thief!' A lady in a voluminous flowery dress, one hand clamping her floppy hat to her head, was sprinting across the field in pursuit of something small and dark that darted amongst the ankles of the crowd.

'Thief!' she repeated.

Zoe recognised the flash of a black beanie hat amongst the sandals and boots. It was Ed, with a box under one arm and a bag in each hand. She jumped from her chair, searching for Ralph. Then she saw him by the entrance to the field. Waiting in his car. Waiting for Ed.

'Stop!' she cried. 'He's got the crown!'

As she raced across the grass, she heard Gordon shout. 'Hey! My money bag – the takings – where's it gone?'

There was a blur to her left. Gordon, she thought? But it was Mr Chuckles. Comedy shoes and nose discarded, he rugby-tackled the chimp.

Zoe saw the scowl on Ralph's face through the car window, his dismissive wave as he revved his engine. His fist slammed against the steering wheel as his tyres whirred uselessly in the mud that had finally seeped back through the sand. There was a noise like the screeching of brakes and suddenly his car was surrounded by braying llamas, the lead one being ridden by the juggler brandishing a burning torch.

It made the front page of the Brascombe Courier. There was talk of a spot on Radio 4. Zoe was just glad it was all over. The crown, the fête takings and an assortment of purses and wallets had been retrieved. She and Gordon had happily handed the matter over to the police.

She had other things to occupy her mind now. Including a date with Charlie Chuckles. He had a real name, Ted Brown, and a proper car. But she had made him promise to take her out in the Bounce-O-Matic as soon as it was fixed. There had to be some perks to going out with a clown.

Aunt Agony

by Helen Kara

Sarah was shattered. A few hours with her 5-year-old nephew, Barney, had turned out to be more stressful than a whole week in her high-powered job. She had no idea why some women wanted to do this with their lives. Children ate up your time and your money, as well as your energy. If she had children, she wouldn't be able to wear her beloved killer heels any more, shop all day with her girlfriends, go out for the night on a whim. She'd probably have loads of wrinkles, too, from all the sleepless nights and no time to go for facials.

Jude, Sarah's sister, loved being a mum, and had never wanted Sarah's help with childcare – which suited Sarah perfectly. Despite their differences, the sisters were great friends. Sarah was also very fond of Jude's husband, Simon, mainly because he made Jude so happy. Which was probably why Sarah had finally agreed to help when, with another baby on the way, Simon had demanded some adult time with Jude before the next round of sleepless nights.

So here she was, being a hands-on auntie for the first time in her life. At least they'd managed to spend the last hour watching *Shaun the Sheep* on DVD, which Barney loved and Sarah thought was very, very boring. She'd been delighted to turn it off and bring Barney upstairs for bedtime. Now he lay curled on his side in his big boy bed, thumb in mouth and eyes half closed.

Sarah reached over to stroke his head. 'Are you ready to go to sleep now, lovey?' she said hopefully.

He pulled his thumb from his mouth. 'You have to read to me, Auntie Sarah,' he said reproachfully, and popped his thumb back in like a punctuation mark.

Oh, bother, did she really? She looked at the bookshelf for inspiration. Something short would be ideal. Then she spotted *Traditional Nursery Rhymes*. Perfect.

'Barney, I'm going to read you some nursery rhymes, okay?'

He looked at her with deep suspicion and pulled his thumb out again. 'I don't go to nursery, I go to big school,' he said.

'I know,' she said hurriedly. 'It's an old time book, your Nanna used to read it to me when I was your age. In those days, 'nursery' just meant something for children.'

Barney didn't look any less suspicious, but his thumb was back in his mouth, and he didn't say anything else. Sarah opened the book at random.

'Georgie Porgie, pudding and pie, kissed the girls and made them cry—'

Barney sat bolt upright. 'Why?'

'Why what?' Sarah was flummoxed.

'Why did they cry when he kissed them? That's silly. Kisses don't hurt.'

She'd forgotten how bright and articulate he was, and knew she wouldn't be able to pull the wool over his eyes.

'No, they don't. But they might not have liked him kissing them.'

Barney looked unimpressed. 'Even if they didn't, they shouldn't cry. They should say bog off.'

'Barney!'

'It should say he *hit* the girls. That would make them cry.' He lay down and popped the thumb back in with a satisfied expression.

'Georgie Porgie, pudding and pie,' Sarah said obediently, 'hit the girls and made them cry. When the boys came out to play, Georgie Porgie ran away.'

Barney nodded happily. 'That's right,' he said. 'Coz he hit the girls, so the boys would hit him if he didn't run away.'

Sarah, worried by all this violence, was searching through the book for a more peaceful rhyme.

'Diddle diddle dumpling, my son John, went to bed with his trousers on.'

She peeked at Barney, whose eyes were round with surprise.

'One shoe off and one shoe on, diddle diddle dumpling, my son John.'

'You haven't got a son,' Barney observed.

'That's right. It's like a story.'

'Where's John's mummy? She should make him wear his pyjamas.'

Sarah spluttered with unexpected mirth. Barney caught her eye and joined in, banging his little fist on the duvet and bellowing with laughter.

'He-he-he-he-he went to bed with his CLOVES on,' Barney chortled, which made Sarah laugh all the more.

When Barney got his breath back, he held out his hand for the book. 'I choose one now,' he announced.

'Okay,' Sarah said. 'Last one, though, all right? Then you go to sleep.'

'Okay,' Barney parroted, leafing through the pages. 'Here.' He held the book out to Sarah, who didn't check to see what he'd chosen, just read:

'Ladybird, ladybird, fly away home. Your house is on fire and your children are gone. All except one, and that's little Ann, because she crept under the frying pan.'

'Where did the children go?' Barney asked anxiously.

'Far away from the fire, so they wouldn't get burned,' Sarah said, in her most reassuring voice.

'So did little Ann get burned?'

'No, she was under the frying pan, remember? You can't get burned under a frying pan.'

'You can't fit under a frying pan,' Barney pointed out.

'A ladybird can, because it's only this big.' Sarah held her finger and thumb close together.

'So how can a ladybird hold a frying pan?'

'They have special ladybird-sized ones,' Sarah said firmly. 'Now it's time for you to go to sleep.'

Barney sat up again, a worried look on his face. 'But if they're special ladybird-sized pans to use, how could she fit underneath?'

'Ladybirds,' Sarah said, fixing Barney with a rapier stare, 'have MAGIC frying pans. They change size to fit what you need them for. If you just need to fry one egg – ladybirds eat ants' eggs – then they're just the right size for that. And if you need to fry a whole breakfast for lots of people, they grow as big as you want. If you have to hide under one, it grows as big as a TENT.'

Barney's eyes were shining with wonder. 'Wowww,' he breathed, and snuggled down on his pillow, thumb back in position.

Sarah stroked his head and kissed him goodnight. She tiptoed from the room, went downstairs and made herself a mug of tea. Jude's squashy sofa was delightfully comfortable. After all the *Shaun the Sheep* episodes, Sarah didn't feel like watching TV. There was a pile of magazines on the coffee table, so she picked one up and began to leaf through it. The knots in her shoulders started to unwind as she brushed up on her knowledge of current fashions.

By the time Sarah finished her magazine, she was feeling much more relaxed. It was only another couple of hours until she would be released from auntie duty, and could go back to her lovely well-organised child-free life. She made herself another cup of tea and leaned back against the sofa cushions. Maybe being an auntie wasn't so bad after all.

Sarah was jolted from her thoughts by a piercing scream.

'Waaaaah! Mumm-eee!'

Help! Now what? She shot up the stairs at high speed.

'Barney, what's wrong?'

He was sitting up in bed, eyes screwed shut, mouth wide open.

'The nightmares are on me,' he howled. 'I want my Mummy, they're running on my skin, make them stop, Auntie Sarah.'

She picked him up, duvet and all, and held him tightly in her arms. 'They've gone away now,' she said, hoping to goodness she was right. 'No nightmares would dare to stick around when I'm here.'

The little body in her arms was shivering with terror. She couldn't leave him like this. Sarah thought wistfully of her tea going cold on the coffee table, and then she had an idea.

'Barney, listen, would you like to come downstairs and

snuggle with me on the sofa?'

He gave a tiny nod and buried his hot head in the crook of her neck. She felt a surge of affection, and settled him more closely in her arms to carry him downstairs. Poor little lad. He couldn't help having a bad dream.

She put him down on the sofa and tucked his duvet around him. 'Better?' she asked, and got another tiny nod in response. 'Look, I'll sit right here by you.'

Barney wriggled as close to her as he could. Sarah looped an arm around him, and he snuggled into her with a big sigh.

I bet I know what would make you feel better, Sarah thought. Can I stand it? She looked down at his tired little face and decided she could.

'Barney, would you like to watch *Shaun the Sheep*?'

His slight smile seemed like a big reward. She reached for the remote and, as the oh-so-familiar music chimed into the room and Barney's body relaxed at last, Sarah realised that he really needed her. Not like a girlfriend might need her to help find the next perfect handbag, or like a work colleague might need her advice on a strategy. Barney needed her to help him through this bit of his life, because he was simply too little to manage on his own. She'd never been needed like that by anyone before. It didn't mean she wanted children, Sarah reminded herself hastily. It wasn't a bad feeling, though.

Sarah looked down at Barney, in the crook of her arm, and saw that he had fallen asleep. The curve of his eyelashes on his cheeks was almost unbearably moving. She could carry him back upstairs, now, and put him into his bed. But she didn't. She sat there with one arm around him, sipping tea, while *Shaun the Sheep* played on.

At Death's Door

by Jill Steeples

'Luce ... Lucy!' Mark's hoarse voice quivered from the bedroom. 'Can you come here a mo, love?'

Sighing, Lucy threw down her magazine, levered herself out of the armchair and traipsed up the stairs. What was it now, she wondered? All day long, she'd been up and down those stairs with steaming mugs of tea, boxes of tissues and painkillers. She'd done the full Florence Nightingale bit, administering ample doses of TLC, but little thanks she'd received in return.

'How're you feeling?' she asked, poking her head round the bedroom door.

'Terrible,' Mark said, blowing his nose noisily into a tissue. 'I feel so weak.' He sniffed from beneath the duvet. 'Perhaps some lightly scrambled eggs might make me feel better.'

'You'd like some eggs?' she said, trying to keep her voice even. 'Right, fine. Eggs it is.'

'And some toast, please,' he called after her departing figure.

What was it with men and colds, she thought, as she stood over the cooker. Absolutely pathetic, the whole lot of them. And Mark was the worst of them all. Such a wuss when it came to illness. Why couldn't he just get on with it, like she'd had to last week when she'd been poorly?

Upstairs, she handed over the tea tray graciously.

'Sorry to be a pain,' Mark croaked, 'but you couldn't just fetch me some ketchup?'

One thing after another, it was. She felt like squirting the sauce all over his blotchy face, but she handed it over with a smile. At least she had her bingo to look forward to. A couple of hours away from Mark and the house would do her the power of good.

As Mark munched heartily through his toast and eggs, Lucy pulled out her sparkly top and cropped trousers from the wardrobe.

'You're not going out tonight?' Mark asked, disbelieving.

She nodded. 'You know Tuesday is my night out with the girls.'

'But, I thought... Oh well,' he said quietly, 'I expect I'll be okay. On my own.'

'Of course you will,' Lucy said, matter-of-factly. 'And I'll only be gone a couple of hours.'

Mark, having finished off all the eggs and toast, put the tray to one side. He then punched his pillows manfully and wrestled with the duvet, sending tissues flying in the air.

'Is it me,' he asked, pathetically, 'or is it warm in here?'

'Look Mark, you haven't got a temperature. I've checked it half a dozen times already.'

'Huh, so why do I feel so dreadful then?'

'It's a cold that's all. The same bug that I had last week. I expect come tomorrow you'll be fine.'

'I don't think it can be the same thing you had. I mean,

you weren't laid up like this, confined to bed, were you?'

Oh, how I wish, thought Lucy. The luxury of spending three days in bed, being waited on hand and foot, was something she could only dream about.

'No, that's true,' she said, with half a smile.

'Perhaps I'll have a bath then. Maybe that'll bring me round. You wouldn't just run it for me before you go?'

She deserved a medal, a badge of honour, for wifely services far and beyond the normal call of duty. Either that or a bit of retail therapy. Yes, definitely that. Tomorrow she'd go shopping and give the joint credit card a bit of a thrashing for her trouble.

The thought immediately made her feel better. She filled the bath to the brim, the foaming bubbles escaping over the side and fetched some new fluffy towels from the airing cupboard.

'Come on then, soldier, your bath's ready,' she called.

'You're not making fun of me, are you?' asked Mark, as he walked gingerly from the bedroom into the bathroom, grabbing her hand for support along the way.

'Would I?' she said with a cheesy grin. 'Just be careful in the bathroom – the floor's a bit wet.'

Lucy watched as he climbed into the bath and eased himself down. He closed his eyes, stretched out his long limbs and luxuriated in the comforting warmth of the water.

'Aw, that's lovely,' he said.

'Good. So is there anything else you need before I go?' she asked, sensing the opportunity to escape.

'No, I don't think so, love. You go. Have a lovely time. And don't you worry about me.'

She had no intention of doing so. She was out to enjoy

herself. Ten more minutes and her lift would be here. Just enough time to clear the mess in the kitchen. She picked up the tea tray and went downstairs.

With any luck, she thought, Mark would be back to normal and back to work tomorrow. Her sympathies were wearing thin and she was looking forward to having the house to herself.

Hearing the tooting of a car horn outside, she grabbed her handbag from the side.

'See you later,' she called up the stairs.

At exactly that moment Mark called out to Lucy, but his faltering voice went unheard. Drat. The shampoo was nestling in the shower beyond his reach. He'd have to get it himself. Feeling weakened by the heat of the bathroom, he steadied himself on the side of the bath, before lifting his leg over the side. But as his foot found the puddle on the vinyl-covered floor, it shot forward. He lost his balance and fell backwards with an ominous thud on to the ground.

'Lu...cy.' He managed a strangled gasp as a single trickle of blood seeped from his head into the pool of water.

As Lucy slammed the door shut, a pang of guilt pricked her conscience. Perhaps she should stay home after all. But when she saw her friend, dressed up to the nines, waving from the car, she thought better of it. Didn't she deserve a bit of fun after the day she'd had? And after all, she told herself, Mark only had a cold. It wasn't as if he was at death's door, was it?

The Green Party

by Tamsyn Murray

'It's very green, Mum. Are you sure it's meant to be that colour?' Sylvia regarded the bowl on the kitchen worktop doubtfully.

Marion gave the gloopy mixture a brisk stir. 'It's lime jelly. What colour do you expect it to be?'

Biting her lip, Sylvia said, 'I don't think Jodie's mother will want her to have any. Too many additives, she'll say.'

'Is she allergic?'

Sylvia shook her head. 'No. Just obsessed with healthy eating.'

'You worry too much,' Marion said. 'No one expects health food at a 5-year-old's party.'

A dark look crossed Sylvia's face. 'You don't know the parents at Kerry's school. Everything has to be organically grown and non-fattening.'

Marion sniffed. 'We're hardly poisoning them, just giving them good old-fashioned party food. I'm sure you're over-reacting.'

Custard the Clown was going down well with the assembled party-goers. They roared with laughter when his voluminous trousers fell down and clamoured for a balloon crown when he presented Kerry with hers.

So far, so good, Sylvia thought as she watched from the living room doorway. In less than an hour, parents would be arriving to collect their offspring and she could heave a sigh of relief that nothing disastrous had happened. The parting comments of Jodie's mother still rang in her ears.

'I didn't know what junk you'd be serving so I brought a packed lunch.' Sylvia had stared, unsure whether to be amused or offended. 'No e-numbers involved.'

Once she'd gone, Sylvia had opened the airtight container and peeked inside. Carrot sticks nestled next to an unappetising brown sandwich. Compared to cakes, crisps and biscuits, the contents of the box seemed wilted and boring. Sylvia began to pity Jodie. The little girl would feel utterly left out when the rest of the children tucked into their party food. Sighing, Sylvia had tucked the box into the fridge and gone through to start Pass the Parcel.

As Custard twisted the last balloon into a puppy, Marion and Sylvia loaded the food onto the dining table and watched with satisfaction as the children tucked in.

'I'd better get Jodie her packed lunch,' Sylvia murmured.

'Packed lunch?' Marion threw her an inquiring look. 'What on earth would she need one of those for?'

Sylvia explained.

'Rubbish!' Marion announced, once she'd finished. 'Jodie can have party food like everyone else. Her mother will never know.'

She strode into the kitchen and seizing the sealed box, she tipped the contents into the bin.

Sylvia groaned and covered her eyes. 'I can't believe you did that.'

Marion smirked in satisfaction. 'Whoops. Silly me, I threw Jodie's packed lunch away by mistake. Now she'll have to eat cakes and crisps.'

The doorbell rang soon afterwards. Sylvia left her mother supervising the children and went to answer it.

'Hi.' A tall, mid thirties man stood there, smiling in a friendly way. 'Is this the right house for Kerry's party?'

Sylvia smiled back, nodding. 'Yes. You're a bit early though.'

He gave a rueful nod. 'I know. My wife is always telling me off for being late so I made a special effort today.' He held out a hand. 'I'm Jodie's dad, Gary.'

Sylvia shook the outstretched fingers then stepped back. 'Sylvia. Why don't you come in?'

As they made their way into the living room, Sylvia took a deep breath. 'There was a mix up with Jodie's packed lunch, I'm afraid.'

Gary frowned. 'Packed lunch?'

'The one your wife gave me.'

A groan escaped him. 'Only Teresa could be that rude.' He shook his head, embarrassed. 'I've told her so many times not to do it, but she refuses to listen.'

'The thing is, we didn't want her to go hungry so we—'

'Daddy!' Jodie ran across the room and wrapped her arms around Gary's knees.

He reached down and swept her up into a hug. 'Hello, sweetheart. Have you had fun?'

Eyes wide, Jodie nodded. 'I saw a big clown and he gave me a balloon and I had some jelly and it was green!'

Sylvia felt her face begin to flush. 'I'm really sorry.'

'Don't apologise, no harm done.' He grinned in conspiratorial fashion. 'To tell the truth, it's not the first time we've disobeyed the Food Police. Jodie and I sometimes have a sneaky ice cream when we're at the park.'

Relief washing over her, Sylvia smiled. 'At least the jelly was green. You could say it was environmentally friendly.'

Gary lowered Jodie to the floor and watched her run to join the other children. 'Eco-jelly? Sounds good to me.' He grinned and an impish gleam crept into his eyes. 'Don't suppose there's any left, is there?'

The Changing World of Michael O'Sullivan

by Kathleen McGurl

Michael O'Sullivan stepped out of his cottage door and breathed in deeply. It was a beautiful June morning and the air sparkled cool and clear. He turned to his left, and then to his right as was his habit, and surveyed the scene he'd lived with all his life. The ridge of Knockowen, craggy and foreboding, gave way to gentle folding hills, then his own pastures, green and fertile, led down to the Glanrastel river in the valley below. He could just make out the twists and turns of the track which led up to his farm. To his right was the rounded hill of Pookeen, tucked in behind was tiny Glanrastel Lough, not visible from the cottage, but it was there, nestled beneath the mountains and teeming with trout, just the same. A mile down the track, a hundred yards off the road, was a stone circle. The valley would hardly have changed since the circle was constructed.

Michael O'Sullivan saw that the world was laid out at his feet. Not for the first time, he considered what he had and counted himself a lucky man.

Later, as he was bottle-feeding the orphaned lamb christened Larry by his wife Aoife, he heard the sound of a car, and stood up to greet his visitors, expecting to see his neighbour Sean MacCarthy, from the farm two miles down the valley. But it was strangers, who'd driven up the long track from the main road. A man and a woman, big, blond and German.

'May we park here, while we walk in your mountains?' asked the man, while the woman clucked at Larry, fondling his ears.

Michael O'Sullivan liked the idea of others enjoying his mountains, and nodded at them. They thanked him and set off, booted and rucksacked.

Four hours later they returned, faces glowing, boots muddy, water bottles empty. Michael O'Sullivan met them as he returned from repairing the fence in the lower fields.

'Excuse me, may we refill our bottles in your kitchen?' asked the man. 'It is a very hot day, no?'

'Sure, and it is that,' replied Michael O'Sullivan. 'But you'll be wanting a cup of tea, not water, I'd say. Can I not ask my wife to put the kettle on for ye?'

Their faces lit up. 'Tea would be, how do you say in this country, *grand*,' replied the man, and the woman smiled.

Aoife, busy in the kitchen making soda bread, seemed pleased to have visitors, and bustled around laying a tray with tea, newly baked bread and a pat of butter, jam, two slices of cake, a jug of milk and a bowl of sugar.

'Michael, fetch those old chairs from the barn, set them in the garden so they can rest their feet, the poor souls. And show them where the bathroom is, they'll be wanting to refresh themselves after their long walk in the hills.'

The German couple sat in the sunshine beside the cottage, drank their tea and ate their bread, complimented Aoife on her baking, used the bathroom, and left a twenty euro note on the chair when they left.

'Sure and wasn't that money for nothing,' Aoife said to her husband that night. 'Couldn't we be serving tea and cake to all our visitors now, it'd bring in a few extra pennies to help when the price of lamb falls again or the EU grants dry up.'

'But you're forgetting that we don't have any visitors. Aren't they the first to come up our road this summer?' Michael protested.

'Michael O'Sullivan, you're as thick as the heel of the bread. You'll be putting a notice down at the gate to advertise, isn't that it now? O'Sullivan's tea rooms – tea, coffee and home baked cakes. We'll get some of those patio tables and chairs for the garden, and polish up the other furniture for the front room in case of rain. We'll charge two euros for a cup of tea and three for a slice of cake.'

The next day Michael O'Sullivan made and painted the sign, while his wife watched over him. He hammered it into the ground, beside the gate where the track left the main road. It was a good spot, the sign would be seen by visitors driving up towards the Healy Pass for the views.

The fine weather continued for another week, unusually for Kerry. And there were five more sets of visitors during that time: all bought tea and cakes, and one family with three children in tow asked for sandwiches and lemonade. Larry was popular with the children, who took turns to feed him, squealing with excitement.

When the weather changed Aoife took the chance to go to town and stock up on sandwich fillings she could freeze, soft drinks in cans, and a coffee filter machine so she could offer the visitors something better than instant.

'Michael, it'll soon be the holiday season. Why don't you ask Sean MacCarthy's boy down below to make you up a leaflet, on that computer yoke he has? You could ask the campsites and B&Bs down along the main road to give them out. A bit of advertising for our tea rooms, like.'

And so it was that throughout the summer there was a steady trickle of visitors on the fine days. Soon enough money had been made to buy the white plastic tables and chairs Aoife had wanted for the garden. All of the visitors seemed to want to climb the hills, and Michael fretted that they'd lose their way if the mist came in. So he painted sticks with red and white stripes, and hammered them into the ground at intervals along the path. He drew a map, which young Gerry MacCarthy put onto the computer and printed out copies for him. And when the visitors arrived, Michael O'Sullivan handed them a map, pointed out and named the mountains, then watched the visitors set off for their hike, thinking not for the first time what a lucky man he was.

One day a couple arrived, parked beside the tumble-down cottage which served as a barn, walked in the hills and left without purchasing so much as a cup of tea. Aoife's face was sour. 'Michael O'Sullivan, we will have to charge them to park here. How else can we cover the costs of printing the leaflets and maps when people like those two take them and buy nothing in return?'

Michael privately thought that the mountains should be free for all to enjoy, but Aoife decided they should charge a euro per car to park. Michael sighed, shrugged, and amended his signs. Aoife also began charging a ten euro fee for those who wanted to fish the plentiful waters of

Glanrastel Lough. Michael worried that they offered little for the younger visitors and busied himself constructing swings and climbing frames in the field adjacent to the garden. And for the older folk who couldn't manage the hills he worked on a riverside path, with a couple of rough log benches he'd made himself set at points along the way.

The next summer trade was brisk. Aoife increased her prices and Michael improved his footpaths and play area. Some visitors complained about the state of the track – the increased traffic was taking its toll. When Sean MacCarthy came to visit he and Aoife discussed whether a grant might be forthcoming from the local council to improve the road, now that they were becoming a tourist attraction. With Gerry MacCarthy's help, a business plan was drawn up and Michael and Aoife took a trip to Tralee to present it to the council officers. By late August the road was complete, and from the door of his cottage Michael O'Sullivan could see it clearly – a black snake winding its way up through the valley. It even had a white line painted along its middle. He missed the twisty potholed old track, but supposed that the new road was an improvement. The council provided new signs too, brown and white, giving directions to 'Glanrastel Country Park' from as far as five miles out. The new name had been Aoife's idea.

Still, every morning, Michael surveyed the scene from his cottage door, noting the tea gardens, play area and neatly laid paths leading people down to the river or across the fields to start the mountain climbs. He thanked God for what he had, and considered he must be a lucky man.

Aoife's next idea was to convert the old cottage into a museum. 'Let's restore it to the way it was when your daddy lived there,' she told Michael. 'Re-thatch the roof, whitewash the walls, and fill it with the old furniture. We'll charge three euros in, or five for a guided tour.'

'Guided tour? And who are you thinking will be conducting them?'

'Why, you of course, Michael O'Sullivan. I have enough to do in the kitchen. I'm going to ask young Grainne MacCarthy to come and help me at the weekends and in the school holidays.'

'But she won't be wanting to make tea and sandwiches all day, a young thing like that!'

'She will if we pay her. Not too much mind, but five euros an hour should do it.'

The next couple of years saw the addition of a tarmac car park; a block of toilets, two for men and two for women; a large septic tank to cope with the increased waste; two quad bikes with a couple of fields set aside for their use; and a new barn. The latter was not for farming use; it contained a second café, an indoor play area, a shop selling trinkets and some pens for the motherless lambs. It blocked the view of Knockowen from the cottage door, but Michael knew, because Aoife had told him, that it was necessary for their growth. Now, Grainne MacCarthy worked full time in the new café, Gerry MacCarthy took care of the park's accounts, and a girl from the village came up to give tours of the cottage and help children feed the lambs.

Aoife noticed how on the hottest days people would bathe in the rock pools of the Glanrastel river. She hired workmen and a bulldozer to redirect some of its water into a dugout pool, with tiled floor, chrome steps and a plastic slide. The river used to gurgle and bubble over a rocky waterfall. Now it was channelled neatly into the pool and on down the valley via large pipes. Michael missed the comforting sounds it had made, but indeed it became a popular attraction.

'Stone circle,' Aoife said to Michael one evening.

'What's that you're after saying?'

'It's too far down the valley. The people park up here, they don't want to be trekking all the way back down there to see it. We'll move it up here, beside the pool.'

'Aoife, my love, we can't be moving the stone circle. Sure, it's an ancient monument!'

'It's on our land, it's not listed by the tourist board, so we can do what we like with it. I'll get Sean MacCarthy to bring his tractor up to shift the stones.'

And so it was done. The stones were set in a neat circle standing in a mowed lawn. A two-foot high plastic leprechaun pointed the way from the car park.

Michael O'Sullivan stepped out of the door of his bungalow and breathed deeply. The septic tank must need emptying soon, he thought. He turned to his left, then to his right, and surveyed the Irish theme park he'd helped to build. He considered what he had, and wondered whether he was indeed a lucky man.

Going Backwards

by Deborah Carr

'No!' shouted Jess, slamming her hands against the steering wheel. 'Not again.' She pushed her sunglasses back into place and turned the key in a vain attempt at starting the engine, knowing full well that if she was going to get to her mother's house at all, it was now going to have to be on foot.

'What's happened, Mummy?' her 3-year-old daughter asked from her car seat in the back, tightly clutching her tatty rag doll.

Jess unclipped her seat belt, forced her mouth into some semblance of a smile and turned to reassure Evie.

'Darling,' she said, patting her daughter's podgy knee. 'It's nothing to worry about. The car has stopped, that's all.'

'But we're not at Grandma's house,' Evie said, staring beyond her mother through the dusty windscreen to the endless fields. 'I'm hot and I want Grandma.'

Jess sighed. 'We're a few miles away, so I'm going to phone Auntie Katy to see if she can collect us,' she said, dragging her handbag from the seat next to her and rummaging amongst the detritus of tissues, make-up and sweet wrappers for her mobile phone. Not daring to think back to the last time she had bothered to charge it, she pulled it out of the bag and held it up. Damn, she thought, her spirits crashing. Flat battery.

'Auntie not there?' Evie asked, a worried expression on her cherubic face as she pushed her thumb into her mouth. It was something she hadn't done for at least six months and it concerned Jess to see her revert to the old habit.

'Probably at the shops,' Jess said, trying to make her voice light. 'Anyway, I think it would be more of an adventure for us to walk there instead. It isn't that far,' she fibbed, gauging that it must be at least five or six miles. 'Won't that be fun?'

Evie nodded silently. Jess could tell she was not convinced.

Pulling her bag strap over her shoulder, Jess lifted Evie onto her hip and checked that the car was locked. She hadn't wanted to return to her home village of Thetson at all – too many memories that she would have preferred not to face – but her mother had insisted. She had told Jess the week before that, as much as she enjoyed visiting her and Evie for the odd weekend, it was about time Jess brought her granddaughter to stay with her, to see her home too.

'Nobody will bother you,' her mother had assured her. 'Your husband walked out on you, that's all. It happens all the time. Anyway, no one really took to him in the first place,' she continued, ignoring Jess's raised eyebrows. 'He was always too big for his boots, wasn't he?'

Jess had given in. How could she admit to her mother that it wasn't the neighbours who concerned her? It was Paul, her childhood sweetheart, the one she had left all those years before without any valid reason at all to try her luck at city living. She had never forgiven herself for hurting him so badly and, now she was in the same position as she had put him in, surely he would be gloating.

‘He would have every right to,’ she mumbled. He was the one person she was avoiding, no one else.

‘Mummy?’ Evie asked, holding on tightly to her mother’s neck.

‘It was nothing, sweetheart,’ she said, realising she must have been muttering out loud. Raising Evie into a more comfortable position on her hip, she wished she had thought to wear trainers, instead of the ballet pumps that were fine for driving and sitting down at her mother’s, but not at all sensible for walking miles on a dusty track.

Within moments, her leg muscles ached and she felt hot and clammy. The path she had taken dipped down through an arch of trees, shading them from the heat of the sun.

‘Sweetheart, you’re going to have to walk for a bit,’ she said, lowering her daughter carefully to her feet, noting that the pathway soon ended and they would be back to walking along the lane once more.

To cheer Evie up, she had begun to sing nursery rhymes, encouraging her to make up new verses for the words, and giggling when Evie teased her with funny tunes. Now she was running out of things to sing about and was getting thirsty. She knew her daughter would soon be, too.

Jess supposed they had covered about a third of their journey, when she saw a car coming towards them. Noticing a lone male in the battered black vehicle, she focused on her daughter and tried not to catch his attention. The car slowed to a stop just past them, and Jess felt her stomach knot with fright when she heard him reversing. Her breath reduced to short, quick pants, she concentrated on remaining calm so as not to let her daughter pick up on her nervousness.

‘Hey there,’ a deep voice shouted.

Jess thought about running, but knew she was too tired to outrun a man, if he chose to chase them. Deciding that she was being melodramatic, she turned to face him, trying her best to look as confident as possible.

'Hello,' she replied.

He leaned closer to his open window, and stared at Jess with an intensity that began to worry her.

'You look as if you could do with a ride,' he said, glancing down to Evie then back to Jess.

'Please don't worry.' Jess cleared her throat and forced a smile. 'Anyway, you're going the wrong way. We're fine.'

'I'll soon turn round,' he said.

'No. Really, we're fine. Thank you.' Jess said, her voice cracking with emotion, as she did her best to look calm. She had heard about dreadful things happening along these lonely roads, and cursed under her breath for being so foolish and not having been organised enough to charge her phone before leaving.

The man's smile had vanished now.

'There's no need to be rude,' he said, his car reversing slowly alongside Jess. She picked up Evie and began to walk as quickly as she could without breaking into a run.

The man opened the car door and started to step out.

'What are you doing?' she said. 'I told you we didn't need a lift.'

'Well, I think you do,' he said, a grin on his sallow face.

Jess put her hand up in a vain effort to stop him moving towards her, turning so that Evie was as far away from him as possible.

'No,' she said, trying her best to take control of the situation. 'Please just leave us alone.'

'Who are you to tell me what to do?' he said, his eyes narrowed to mere slits.

He was closer to them now and Jess could smell stale sweat and cigarette smoke. For a moment she froze, thinking of Evie. Should she tell her to run and stay and fight him herself? But Evie was only three. What could she do to save her daughter?

As a dirty hand reached towards her she screamed.

'Hey! Get away from her!' shouted a deep voice she vaguely recognised.

The stranger immediately strode back to his car, slammed the door and drove off quickly.

'Jess? Is that you?'

Jess had been unaware of another car pulling up behind her, but instantly recognised the man who now stepped out of it. It was the one person she had been hoping to avoid, but all she felt was relief.

'Paul?' she asked, noting he didn't seem surprised to see her so unexpectedly.

'Thank God you're all right,' he said, stepping out of the car. 'Your mum was getting a little worried that you two hadn't arrived at her house. She asked me if I'd take a quick drive and have a look to see if I could find where you'd got to.'

'She's always telling me off for not sorting out my car,' Jess replied. 'I'm sure I don't have to tell you how relieved I am to see a friendly face right now.'

Paul glanced down the road and shook his head, his expression angry.

'I got his number plate. I'll give the police a call just as soon as we get you home. Just as well your mum is such a persuasive woman,' he said, looking at Evie, her head resting on her mother's shoulder. 'You're looking well, Jess. Motherhood suits you.'

Jess hoped he would mistake the redness of her cheeks as heat from exertion rather than embarrassment of meeting up with someone she had once shared so many dreams with.

'Thanks.' She wished she had taken a little more effort with her appearance before leaving home that day. She tried not to stare at him, but could not ignore how the once scrawny teenager she had loved and left was now a man with whom she was more than happy to be reacquainted.

He cleared his throat bringing her back to the present.

'Why don't I take you both to your mum's place and maybe tomorrow I'll come back and see if I can sort out your car?' he said, holding the door open for her.

Jess nodded. She could not help wondering how he could be so forgiving when she'd left him so abruptly all those years ago. Especially when she had gone without even leaving him a note of explanation.

How cruel she'd been to him. Her mother had written her several letters angrily describing how lost Paul had been after her disappearance. In fact, it had been a relief when her mother had told her of his engagement to someone they both knew from college. Knowing he'd moved on from their relationship had helped her feel a little less guilty about being so selfish.

'That would be great, thanks. It's too hot to be carrying a toddler for miles, and she's quite a bit heavier than she looks,' she said, helping him strap Evie into the back of the car.

Paul started the engine as soon as they were seated. Turning to face Jess, he said, 'It's good to see you again.'

'You, too,' she admitted, unable to help thinking how right it felt being with him after so long.

'I almost bumped into you last July.' Paul smiled, but kept his focus on the road.

Jess frowned. She didn't recall seeing him in London. 'You did? Where?'

'I was leaving a restaurant when I heard your laugh. You came round the corner and I had to step out of the way to avoid you.'

'Why didn't you say something?'

Paul tilted his head thoughtfully. 'I was going to, but there was a man right behind you. I assumed he was your husband. He was pushing this little lady in her buggy.'

Jess remembered that day only too well. Her husband had insisted they spent a weekend seeing the sights. She stared out of the window thinking how ignorant she had been about his imminent plans to leave her and Evie. How could he have given them such a perfect weekend and left days later without a backward glance?

Jess turned and studied Paul's profile. Did he know what had happened? Did he think, as her mother had done, that her husband's treatment of her was payback for what she had done to Paul?

'I've never apologised for leaving without saying goodbye, have I?' Jess knew her apology was long overdue.

'You don't have to.' He shrugged. 'I was a bit shell-shocked at the time and I'm sure you heard about my rebound relationship.'

Jess nodded. 'Mum told me. How is Carol?'

'Happily married, and living in Toulon, or so I last heard.'

'Oh.' Jess didn't know what to say.

Paul laughed. 'Don't look so concerned. You did me a favour, although I didn't know it at the time.'

'How?' Jess couldn't wait to hear what he had to say.

'If you hadn't left, you would have been miserable. And it made me realise that there's more to life than hanging about Thetson, however pretty it may be. I followed my dream, like you did, and went to live in the States for a few years.'

'But you came back here to live?'

'Yes. Once I'd made my contacts it didn't matter where I worked, thanks to the Internet, and here still felt like home after all. So you have nothing to apologise to me for.' He slowed to allow a tractor to pass by. 'Staying long?' He smiled.

'I'm not sure,' she replied, feeling freed from the guilt that had niggled at her for so long and wondering if she detected the hint of a dare in his question. 'But you're right about it feeling like home.'

Maybe going backwards to revisit her past had not been such a bad idea after all.

From Tesco's With Love

by Sally Quilford

Kelly was in the supermarket when the truth came to her, set free by the array of notebooks for children, labelled to guide young people to their proper roles in life. On one side of the shelf were the girls' books, decorated with Barbies, pink kittens or rabbits. Life for them would be filled with pink and fluffy memories, leading them safely to womanhood and the domestic sphere. The boys' were in camouflage patterns, and had '*Top Secret – For Your Eyes Only*' stamped on them in faded ink, guiding young men to heroic pursuits, protecting Queen, country, and the fluffiness of womanhood from the dark side of life.

She rushed home, checking that no one followed her. Now she knew the truth, she realised someone else had to know it too. All those years wasting her time washing socks and attending school plays. She could have been off doing exciting things.

As she walked along her street, a man came running out of a house. Kelly burst into action, chasing him and throwing him to the ground in the middle of the road.

'Who are you, and what are you doing?' Kelly straddled him and squeezed his neck with nimble fingers.

'I... er... I'm Geoff, from number ten,' he croaked. 'The chip pan caught fire and I was trying to escape. The firemen are on the way.'

Kelly looked back and saw smoke billowing from Geoff's hallway.

'Well,' she said, getting up. 'Don't do it again!'

At dinner that evening, she waited until her husband, James, and her step-children, Holly and Felix, had finished eating.

'I've got something to tell you all.'

'What is it, love?' asked James.

'I realised something today that's going to be a shock to you. There's no easy way to say it... but I'm not really Kelly Phillips, housewife and mum. My name is Lana Anderson and I'm a secret agent.'

James, Holly and Felix looked at her, their mouths agape, and then they looked at each other and burst out laughing.

'Good joke, love, but it's not April Fools' Day yet.'

'I'm not joking. I remembered when I was in Tesco's today. I realise it's going to be difficult, but I can't just stay here and be a mum now I know the truth. My job is to save the world from evil dictators and rich men intent on stealing all the gold and diamonds.'

'Are you going away, Mum?' said Holly, her big blue eyes filling with tears.

For the first time since she'd realised, Kelly felt bad about her decision. She didn't know if she'd had some drugs given to her to make her forget and that these included fooling her into thinking she loved this family, but she did have strong feelings for them. She decided she must be one of those secret agents with a conscience, who cared about good people, but didn't mind beating ten shades of stuffing out of the bad guys.

'It isn't safe for me to stay, darling,' she said to Holly. 'People might hurt you to get to me. That's how these things happen. They'll take you hostage and make me set off a nuclear bomb or something. Then I'll have to rush around saving you, before stopping them setting off the bomb. I'm a woman, so I can multitask if needs be, but it will be traumatic for you and Felix.'

'You're serious, aren't you?' said James. 'I think maybe you need to speak to someone, love. A doctor or something.'

'I am not mad, Jim. I know who I really am. I even remember the things I've done. The places I've been. Posh hotels, with jacuzzis and handsome bellboys on tap. Being dangled over a pit of tarantulas by a villain and escaping just in time to stop him blowing up Milton Keynes. I can't live here now that I know there are so many bad guys out there. It's possible they even put me in this state so I'd be out of action.'

'So you think me and the kids are a part of the conspiracy?'

'No, don't be silly. I remember us meeting and falling in love.'

'Let's get the kids to bed and we'll talk about this, okay?' said James. 'Come on, kids, I'll make you some cocoa.'

Kelly tucked Holly and Felix in, and kissed them goodnight. 'I do love you both,' she said. 'And I am sorry I won't be your mum anymore.'

When she got downstairs, there were two glasses of red wine on the coffee table.

'Come and have a drink and we'll work out what we can do,' said James. 'Maybe you can have your career as a super spy, in between school runs.'

'You're making fun of me, because you think I'm having a nervous breakdown,' she said, sitting down next to him on the sofa. As he moved closer to her, she knew she would miss him too. She kissed him.

'Hmm, I'll definitely miss that if you go,' he said. 'Drink up. We'll go upstairs and say goodbye properly.'

Hours later, Kelly dozed in James' arms, thinking that life in the suburbs with a handsome husband and two lovely kids wasn't the worst thing in the world.

At around three in the morning she heard a noise and opened her eyes to see Geoff, the neighbour, standing over James, pumping a syringe full of fluid into his arm. She tried to move, tried to speak, but found she couldn't do either.

'I'm not stupid, Lana,' said Geoff. 'I drugged you first. I knew you'd found out the truth when you jumped me and it wouldn't be long before you realised who I was. You're lucky I can't stand blood. You, hubby and the children will soon return to blissfully ignorant domesticity. You won't remember a thing.'

One Day at a Time

by Tamsyn Murray

'Becky! We're going to be late!' Simon bellowed up the stairs, hoping his daughter would hear his frustration and get a move on. It was a long shot, he had to admit. They'd been last in at the school gates every day this week, earning him searching looks from Rebecca's teacher. Yesterday, she'd taken him to one side, asked softly if she could do anything to help. Subduing a familiar wave of panic, Simon had responded with a gruff shake of his head and mumbled an excuse about car trouble. Afterwards, he'd been ashamed of the lie, but the teacher had been trying to be kind and that was the last thing he felt able to cope with.

Becky materialised at the top of the stairs and thundered down to the hallway, accompanied by a jumble of cardigan, school bag and shoes.

'Move, Daddy! I need to get to the mirror.'

The breath caught raggedly in Simon's throat as she pushed past him. She reminded him so much of Miranda: a seven year old version of what he'd lost. Others had assured him time would heal, but when? Six months after his wife's death he was still waiting for the aching hole to start to mend and all the while his memories of her grew tarnished.

At least he had Becky, although her likeness to her mother often hurt.

'Where's your coat?' His voice sounded thick to his ears, but Becky seemed not to notice. Her tongue stuck out as she concentrated on stretching a hair bobble around her blonde ponytail.

'In the kitchen. I can't find my pencil case, I think it might be on the table.'

Anxious to avoid another sympathetic look from Miss Charles, Simon hurried to the kitchen. The coat was there, hanging on the back of a chair. The missing pencil case was beside it, where Becky had left it after doing her homework. He gathered up both, then paused. A mug bearing the slogan 'World's Greatest Mummy' sat on a coaster near their dirty breakfast dishes. He frowned. It hadn't been there earlier. Becky must have got it out; the second time this week that had happened. Picking it up with reverent hands, he restored it to the safety of the cupboard. He would have to talk to her about it. They had rules about playing with Mummy's things.

Reaching the weekend was a blessed relief, Simon acknowledged as he collected Becky from the playground that afternoon. He could look forward to two whole days without his colleagues treading on eggshells around him, terrified of saying the wrong thing and reminding him that Miranda was dead, as if he ever forgot.

Sue from Accounts had been collecting for 'Wear It Pink' day today. The rattle of the collecting tin and her cajoling voice reached him long before she'd arrived in the doorway of his office. Horrified, her hand had covered her mouth as she'd backed away, stuttering meaningless apologies. Simon had considered going after her, to tell her it was okay. Instead, he'd turned dull eyes back to his computer screen and noted there were still three hours until he could pick up his daughter and hide away from the world again.

Becky was chattering ceaselessly, telling him about her day. He smiled in the right places, nodded absently when she asked a question, but her actual words passed him by. It took a moment to realise she was tugging at his hand.

'Daddy? Will you sort it out with Courtney's mummy, then?'

Simon followed her pointing finger and saw a dark haired woman stood hesitantly some distance away across the playground. His first instinct was to turn tail and flee, but it was too late, she'd seen him notice her. She approached, smiling as she got closer.

'Mr Knowles?' The woman's voice was soft, obviously worried she was intruding. 'I'm Lucy, Courtney's mum. She's in the same class as Becky at school. I – well – we, really, wondered whether Becky would like to come round and play one day after school?'

Trying to block out the sudden roaring sound in his ears, Simon could only stare. Let Becky go to someone else's house? No, he wouldn't be able to bear it. It was as much as he could stand to leave her at school each day, knowing only a few short hours had to pass before he could sweep her into the security of his arms. Becky was all he had left of Miranda. He couldn't risk anything happening to her.

Lucy was still talking, oblivious to his mounting panic. 'It would be no trouble and I thought it might give you a bit of time to yourself, in case you have things you need to do.'

Simon felt himself backing away. 'It's very kind, but I don't think we can. Becky isn't ready, it's too soon.'

He caught a glimpse of the woman's consternation and fled abruptly, tugging an upset Becky behind him. It wasn't until they reached the sanctuary of the car that he turned to her, gently wiping away the streaks left by her tears and willing her to understand.

'Why can't I go to Courtney's? Her mum asked you really nicely.' Becky screwed up her face, bursting out, 'We never do anything anymore. Stacy's going to Chessington this weekend. I want to go there too!'

He held her as she sobbed, her small fists beating painlessly against his chest whilst he stared over her head. Vaguely, he registered Courtney's mother pass by, her eyes fixed on the ground. She had meant well, he knew. It was just too soon.

Later, once Becky was asleep and he was slumped in front of the muted TV, Simon replayed the event in his mind. Was he being unfair to Becky in his need to keep her close? At the bereavement group he'd attended once, someone had suggested he talk to his wife as though she was still there, out of sight, but within hearing. He hadn't seen the point; Miranda would never answer him. What was the use in speaking to her?

Wearily, he passed a hand across his eyes. It was all so overwhelming; there were so many things he didn't know how to deal with. Maybe getting a few worries off his chest would help.

'Becky was invited round to someone's house today,' he began haltingly, his voice echoing around the empty living room. 'I said no. I mean, I don't know the woman.' A thought occurred to him. 'You might have done though. Lucy, I think she said her name was.'

The words came more easily. Before he knew it, he was talking about Becky's recent parent's evening, the badge she'd got for swimming fifty metres at the local pool, the upcoming birthday party of a friend that he couldn't face going to alone. Words spilled out and with them came all the emotions he'd been holding in for months. Tears rolled down his cheeks and he began to sob uncontrollably.

'It's so hard, Miranda. I miss you and I can't do this on my own.' His fist smashed into a cushion on the sofa beside him. 'I need you. Why did you have to leave me?'

Simon awoke early the next morning with swollen eyes and a thumping headache. He stared at the bedroom ceiling for a few minutes before dragging back the duvet and making his way downstairs in search of paracetamol. It was a pity it only dealt with physical pain, he thought, as he washed a couple of tablets down with some water from the fridge.

Last night's dinner plates were still on the table. Without much interest, he began to load them into the dishwasher. He paused when his hand settled on what looked like a clean mug. It was Miranda's. His eyes flicked to the closed cupboard above the kettle. He was certain he'd put it away yesterday, after he'd spoken to Becky about handling Mummy's things.

'But I didn't touch it, Daddy. I didn't!'

She had still been asleep when he'd checked on her minutes earlier. The mug had been safely in the cupboard when he'd gone up to bed last night. A frown creased his forehead. It must be Becky. There was no other possible explanation. Unless...

Scarcely able to credit what he was thinking, Simon took in a shallow breath and picked up the mug. He slid it onto the shelf, closing the door with both hands. Then he made his way to the living room sofa, perching on the edge and resting his hands tensely on his knees. He was being a fool. Was he seriously expecting his dead wife to take her mug from the cupboard? And what did it mean if she did?

Unable to wait any longer, he strode back to the kitchen, pausing uncertainly at the closed door. Please, he prayed in desperation. *Please let it be her.*

Swallowing hard, he pushed the handle down and gazed into the room. Instantly, his legs turned to jelly and he clutched at the doorframe for support. The mug rested in exactly the same place as earlier. Simon sank to his knees, tears welling up into his eyes. His wild, crazy hope had been rewarded; she hadn't left him after all.

It was raining on Monday afternoon when Simon made his way into the playground. More than once, he dodged sideways to avoid an oncoming umbrella. No one gave him a second glance. They were all too intent on staying dry until they could scurry back to the warmth of their homes.

The classroom door opened and the children's voices filled the air. Becky was the last to come out, chatting animatedly to another girl with coffee-coloured skin. It took Simon a moment to realise that it was the child from last Friday. Coldness clutched at his stomach. That meant her mother must be nearby. He hoped she wouldn't try to speak to him again.

Skipping towards him, Becky slid her hand into his. She turned her face up to him and flashed her mother's smile. For once, it didn't fill him with the ache of loss. Since Saturday morning he hadn't been quite so alone. As irrational as it sounded, he felt like Miranda was somehow nearer.

Feeling someone watching him, he raised his head. Lucy was gazing in his direction, clearly trying to work out whether she should approach him. Simon threw up a brief prayer to his wife and started to cross the playground.

He pasted a wobbly but determined smile upon his face. 'Hi, I'm Simon. I wondered whether your offer for Becky to come over after school was still open?'

Picture Perfect

by Jenny Maltby

As the doorbell rang, I picked up the photo of Luc and smiled ruefully at him. 'See you later,' I told him before sliding him face down on top of the bookshelf.

I didn't want to go out. I never wanted to go out, not really. I much preferred my own little world, closing the front door behind me after work and curling up under a heavy blanket with a microwave meal and a soppy film. But Andrea had refused to take no for an answer this time.

'Won't be a sec,' I shouted down the hall. I always kept Luc's photograph somewhere nearby. It's one of those pictures where the eyes always seem to follow you, no matter where you are in the room. Well, one eye to be exact. I'm not sure what happened when the photo was taken, but half his face is obscured, blending into the dark corner of wherever it was taken. It captured his cheeky, chipped tooth grin though, that's for sure.

Andrea looked me up and down. 'Hmmm, not bad,' she allowed. 'I think you'll do.'

'I'm only coming out to stop you hassling me – and on the condition that you do not, under any circumstances, chat up any men on my behalf. Got it? Honestly, it was so embarrassing last time.'

Andrea laughed, shaking her head in despair. 'Carrie, you've got to get back on the dating trail. You're lovely, you're pretty – there's some guy out there who's perfect for you, just wait and see.'

We'd been best friends since school and I couldn't remember a time when she didn't have a boyfriend to chatter about. We were now twenty years down the road – a dusty, single lane track in my case. And now that she was married to Mark, she seemed all the more determined to find me a husband too, no matter how much I protested.

'I'm perfectly happy on my own. The last thing I need is another one of your schemes to find me a man.' I peered over my specs, not needing to remind her of the several appalling blind dates she had fixed up for me.

'Hey, there was nothing wrong with David. Tall, dark and house-trained – what more could any girl want?'

I knew what I wanted and his name was Luc. I smiled to myself and imagined him padding about barefoot in his faded jeans, coffee gurgling in the pot as he made it just the way I liked on a Sunday morning. He was great in the kitchen, like a TV chef, rustling up just the right thing out of nowhere, despite my constant lack of decent ingredients. A French, guitar-strumming, culinary magician. That's what I needed. He was just too good to be true.

Andrea smoothed her hair in the hall mirror. 'Come on, time to go. You're going to have fun if it kills you! And if you don't put your happy face on, I'm booking you in for speed dating.'

She didn't give up easily. I'd even let her talk me into internet dating once. 'Male order,' Andrea called it.

Nightmare. It reminded me of shopping at Tesco on a Saturday afternoon: too many people in a hurry to find what they wanted, but making do with the bargains on offer.

So this was it – a night out in the local wine bar. Real people and real flirting. I'd made the required effort – anything to stop Andrea getting any more hi-tech dating ideas. Grey hairs blended in, skin mud-packed, clothes starved into for two days. Andrea was right though – I really didn't look too bad at all.

Thackerays was packed, people spilling out through the doors into the small, enclosed courtyard where tiny lights twinkled in trees. I'd forgotten how good it was to be out and about, surrounded by chatter and laughter; even the thud of the music pulsed pleasantly through me. I felt part of real life. Smiling, I made my way through the bank of bodies towards the bar, swooshing my special-occasion dangly earrings against my neck. As someone pushed past me I glanced to the side, wondering whether my new Hi-Shine Hazel hair would be shimmering in the light, as promised on the box.

I gasped. No! It couldn't be! On the other side of the bar was that wonky, French-accented smile I knew so well. I stood there like an idiot, open-mouthed, oblivious now to the noise and pushing and shoving. I couldn't move, even when the colour rushed to my face as he looked up and caught me standing there, my eyes boring into him and my mouth gawping.

When the photo had fallen out of the library book, it hadn't occurred to me that he might actually be real, living in this town. I had simply dreamt up who I thought he might be, breathing life into him and building my daydreams around him. But now, there he was – all of him! Both eyes, too.

I'd imagined him close to me, whispering sexily in my ear, ''Ello, 'ow are you my cherie?' Things like that. I know, it's pathetic. It would have been laughable had he not been making a beeline for me.

Just like in all those crazy daydreams, he leant in towards my neck. I could feel his breath on my cheek and just made out his words over the loud music.

'Allreet Pet? What's a nice lass like you doing in a place like this then?'

It probably wasn't the reaction he was hoping for, but I burst out laughing. It broke the ice at least. He wasn't called Luc, of course. He was Stuart. And yes, we got on brilliantly. After our first proper date a few days later, I went back to his place for coffee. Well, I couldn't have him back to my flat, could I? How would I ever have explained having his photograph on my mantelpiece already?

Out of the Frying Pan

by Leigh Forbes

Becky was still settling Alfie in his cot when she got the first hint that all was not well downstairs. Fortunately, she had already decided that her little bundle of irritability was not going to produce a burp, and had put him down as he was. With her son's thumb plugging his mouth, and the sharp smell of burning onions stinging her nose, Becky made a dash for the kitchen.

She was still staring at the blackened mess in the frying pan when her husband wandered into the room.

'Oh, Justin, you could have given them a stir.'

Justin gazed blankly at the hob. 'Sorry, love. I was changing.' He pulled a bottle of wine from the rack, the clunking of glass belying his calmness. 'One glass or two?'

'Very funny,' she said, and scraped the charred remains into the bin. 'It's a good job I have another onion.'

'Don't you think you ought to put a frock on? They'll be here soon.'

'Well, yes, obviously. But I've got to get this going, or we'll be eating pizza for dinner.'

Becky set the other onion sizzling. 'Now, can you watch this for me, while I get changed?' she said, hauling her apron strap over her head. 'Just give it a stir every few minutes, and if it looks like it's burning, take it off the heat.' She took a slug of wine from the glass Justin handed her. 'Okay?'

'I'm sure I can manage to fry an onion, love.'

Becky wasn't confident that Justin could manage anything just now, not with Anthony Viccari coming to dinner. She knew her husband's chances of being taken on as a junior partner would be greatly improved if he could impress the senior partner, but for a bangers-and-mash girl, who lived in jeans and jumpers, and thought Saturday evenings were for lounging on the sofa watching TV and eating Margheritas, this dinner party was already proving to be a challenge.

Upstairs, she took her new dress down from the back of the bedroom door and admired its subtle shimmer, its understated style, its elegance. Bought the previous week in the town's finest boutique, she had singled it out as the one most likely to impress Anthony, or, more importantly, Anthony's wife. Though she knew nothing about Caroline Viccari, other than that she ate bad dressers for lunch.

The phone rang, and Justin's voice wafted up the stairs. 'Yes, okay. If you've reached the level crossing, you're nearly here. Keep going until you get to the pub, then after a hundred yards you come to a...'

Becky's panic rose as she listened. If Anthony and Caroline had reached the crossing, they were barely two miles away. They were early.

Tugging off her clothes, she struggled frantically into her dress. Not bad, she thought, glancing in the mirror. All those postnatal sit-ups had been worth it. Now, what about the rest of her? Face? Okay; it had had the works earlier. Hands? Ditto. Hair? A handful of mousse and a blast of the dryer would have to do now.

Hair sorted, she had just enough time to smudge on some make-up before the sound of a car door closing dragged her to the window. Outside, she saw a starched man in his fifties walk around the back of a brand new Mercedes and open the passenger door. The woman Becky supposed to be Caroline stepped out.

For two seconds, Becky's heart stopped beating, and a vacuum formed in her chest while she waited for it to start again. When it did, it hammered at twice the pace. She glanced down at her beautiful new dress, noting again its shimmering hues. Then she looked back at the woman walking towards her house.

Caroline Viccari was wearing The Same Dress.

Becky leapt away from the window and stood, hand on chest, searching the room as though the answer might jump out at her. Well, it wouldn't be jumping out of the wardrobe; little more than jeans and baggy jumpers in there. She had the odd nice frock, as Justin called them, but nothing else that would satisfy Caroline Viccari's notorious appetite for style.

She began a frantic rummage, while downstairs the door knocker sounded like a death knell through the house.

Becky pulled out what Justin referred to as her earth-mother dress. With its acres of flowing fabric, it had been a present from her sister-in-law. Becky had always thought it made her look like a gypsy dancer, but further inspection of the cupboard confirmed that it was either that, or her mother's kilt. Everything else was in the wash or buried in the long-forgotten ironing pile.

Peeling off her boutique dress, Becky hauled on the other, and immediately remembered why it lived at the far end of the cupboard. The fabric had that irritating quality to it, as though it were woven from a million tiny pine-needles. She scratched absent-mindedly at her neck and checked herself in the mirror. Frumpy, but smart enough.

It was then she smelled burning.

She flew down the stairs, catching only a fleeting glimpse of two beautiful people in the lounge, and straight into the kitchen. The frying pan contained yet another blackened mess. Justin appeared at the door.

'Oh, hello, darling. Come and say hello to Anthony and Caroline.'

Her mind a conflict of recriminations and recovery plans, not to mention the urge to scratch all over, she followed her husband through to the other room. Attack, she had decided, would be the best form of defence. Don't slurp your wine, she told herself. Remember to smile. And don't scratch.

'How lovely to meet you,' she strode towards her guests and shook their hands, 'And Caroline, what a beautiful dress.' A couple of sizes larger, she noted with satisfaction, but definitely the same.

Caroline stroked the fabric covering her hip. 'Thank you.' Her eyes flicked over the long folds of Becky's skirts, her lips thinning into what might have been a smile. 'And yours, it's—'

'And those earrings,' Becky said. 'They're beautiful too. Are they emerald?'

Caroline's eyes narrowed perceptibly. 'Green sapphire, actually.'

'And such a beautiful pendant to match. How lovely.'

Caroline frowned. 'Well, of course...'

'Don't you need to do something with supper?' Justin

cocked his head dramatically towards the kitchen. 'You asked me to remind you.'

Becky forgave him on the spot. 'Yes. That's right.' She turned to Caroline, adding, 'if you'll just excuse me...' an onion-recovery plan forming as she scarpered.

'It's me,' she hissed into the phone a minute later. 'Have you got an onion?'

Her neighbour had two onions, she learned, ready and waiting for collection. Becky slipped out of the house, and through the hole in the hedge. Unfortunately, she also slipped on the wet grass on her way back, and slid down the bank on her bottom. Legs flailing.

'Nooooo,' she cried, twisting to inspect the back of her dress. As earthy as it was, the grass stain just didn't blend in, and nor did the mud.

She crept into the kitchen, hurriedly set another onion going, and snuck back up the stairs.

What now?

Becky groaned, remembering Caroline's perfectly coiffed hair and flawless face, and tried to weigh up the severity of offence – in fashion terms – of her mother's kilt, versus jeans. A lull in conversation downstairs alerted her to the need for speed. The kilt won.

She cast off the earth-mother dress, and pulled on the kilt. She found a plain blouse and some pretty necklaces, and made another inspection in the mirror. The overall effect was not boutique beautiful, or even earth-mother modest, but it was passable. And it was time to stir the onion.

Her foot had reached only the second step down when Alfie's I-need-attention-NOW wail suddenly kicked in at full volume.

Becky groaned and slid in to his room. He lay on his back, his little fists clenched as tightly as his eyes. Only his mouth was open, displaying a black, gaping hole of pure noise. She picked him up quickly, and settled him against her shoulder. 'There, poppet,' she said. 'Have you got a burp for mummy now?'

It took a good few minutes of leg kicking, gurgling, and pulling at Becky's hair before Alfie obliged with a loud belch. 'Right,' she said, kissing his forehead. 'Back to bed with you.'

With Alfie settled again, Becky eased his door closed, and turned to go back downstairs. A faint smell reached her, bearing with it the news of her latest onion's demise.

'Anything I can do?' Justin called as she breezed past the living room door.

'No, thank you. Everything's fine.'

With the fourth onion peeled (as was her self-confidence), chopped (along with a bit of her finger), and frying gently (just like her nerves), Becky refilled her glass, emptied it, refilled it, and ventured into the living room. She sat primly next to Justin on the sofa, resisting the temptation to slouch back into the cushions.

Caroline raised an eyebrow. 'Weren't you wearing something else just now?' Her eyes ranged down to Becky's legs. 'Is that a kilt?'

'Yes, it was my mother's,' Becky said airily. 'It must be an antique now. Real wool, you know? Yards of it. Very warm in the middle of a Scottish winter, I'm told. Bit hot for the summer, of course, but they're designed to cope with arctic winds blowing in off—'

'Er, Becky, love,' Justin said. 'Alfie's... er... left a little something just here.' He pulled a hanky from his pocket, and began dabbing at the back of her shoulder.

Becky forced herself to keep looking straight ahead. 'Excuse me,' she said through a forced smile. 'Must just go and check the... er... supper.' She edged backwards around the sofa, praying that her smile was brighter than her cheeks, and made another hasty exit.

Back in the safety of her bedroom, she twisted round to see herself in the mirror and tried not to cry. The tell-tale milky splat stretched from shoulder to hip. She clenched her fists in frustration and let out a long moan. She loved her husband, and worked so hard at supporting his career, but she hated dinner parties, and she hated fancy food. And she hated dressing up. And no one could say she hadn't tried.

There was only one thing for it.

Five minutes later, Becky sauntered into the living room wearing her favourite jeans and frumpy jumper, complete with frayed cuffs, and plonked herself on the sofa. She smiled brightly at Caroline's astonishment and said, 'Bit of a wardrobe disaster, I'm afraid. And...' she sniffed the air. 'Judging by the smell coming from the kitchen, bit of a culinary one too. And this time I fear it's terminal. Take-away pizza anyone?'

'Oh, thank goodness for that.' Anthony beamed and loosened his tie. 'I thought you were going to be all fancy food and stiff manners.'

Ignoring his wife's glare, and undoing his top button, Anthony took the take-away menu Becky offered him.

'Pizza's just great, thanks,' he said. 'As long as it doesn't have any onion on it. I can't stand onions.'

The Woman in White

by Jill Steeples

It was on the third day of their holiday that Sarah and Brett first saw the woman in the white dress. They'd spent the morning exploring the castle ruins up on the hill. It was something Sarah had done many times as a child with her parents, but seeing it with Brett, through a fresh pair of eyes, was like discovering it for the first time all over again. Afterwards, they'd wandered hand in hand down the cobbled alleys into town, looking in the windows of the art galleries and gift shops as they passed, commenting on the funny postcards and silly souvenirs.

When they reached the main square, Sarah felt as if she'd come home. The old buildings, the cafés and shops were all comfortingly familiar. Highcliffe was one of her very favourite places, one she associated with happy memories and one she could never imagine growing tired of.

'So what's it to be then?' asked Brett. 'An ice cream, or tea and cakes?'

'Um, decisions, decisions,' sighed Sarah, longingly. 'How about tea and cakes, then? We could always manage to squeeze in an ice cream later.'

'Good idea,' said Brett, grinning.

As they meandered through the throng of sightseers, a peculiar feeling overcame Sarah. Something made her stop and look over her shoulder to the other side of the square. She gasped, causing Brett to stop abruptly.

'Oh my goodness,' she cried, her hand flying to her mouth. 'Look over there, at that woman!'

Brett was already transfixed. He let out a strange, hollow laugh as he looked from the woman to Sarah.

'How funny,' he said, grabbing Sarah tighter by the hand.

The woman was wearing a long flowing white skirt and matching tunic, but in all other respects she was the walking double of Sarah. The same willowy build, auburn hair that fell in soft waves to her shoulders and distinct, defined features could leave no one in any doubt that the two women must be related in some way. Identical twins, even!

'Well, they say everyone's got a double,' laughed Brett, 'and I think she could be yours. Fancy that, two gorgeous women in the same town. How lucky can one guy get?'

But Sarah wasn't laughing. The colour had drained from her cheeks and her hands shook uncontrollably.

'She's looking at me,' Sarah said. 'I think she's trying to tell me something. She's pointing at something, over there. What can it be?'

'Come on, let's go and see,' said Brett, taking control. 'I expect she's as surprised as you are bumping into her look-alike.'

Sarah stood on the spot, reluctant to move.

'I'm not sure,' she said. 'I've got a bad feeling about this.'

'Oh don't be silly,' said Brett. 'We'll go and introduce ourselves.'

As he took her by the arm, a caterpillar of school

children, the girls in pretty gingham dresses and the boys in grey shorts and blue polo shirts, crossed in front of their path, and for a moment Sarah and Brett's attention was diverted by their noisy chatter. When they looked up, to where the woman had been standing, she'd gone. They looked all around them, to every corner of the square, but there was no sign of her anywhere.

'She's obviously done a runner,' joked Brett. 'Can't say I blame her. It isn't every day you come face to face with a living image of yourself.'

'My doppelganger,' said Sarah, solemnly, before tears fell down her cheeks. 'And what was it she was trying to tell me? She was pointing over there, towards the sea.'

Brett looked at Sarah and saw the fear in her eyes. He pulled a tissue from his pocket and dried her eyes.

'She probably wasn't even looking at us at all. It was probably her friend or boyfriend behind us. That's where she's gone, to find them, onto the beach.'

Later when they were sitting outside a café, Sarah found her appetite for cake had vanished. Instead, she sipped pensively at her tea.

'It's supposed to be unlucky to see your doppelganger,' she said, looking up into Brett's eyes. 'An omen of your own...'

Brett shook his head. 'Come on now, that's just a silly myth. Besides, I'm sure if we'd got up close to her, she probably wouldn't have looked anything like you.'

But, despite Brett's reassurances, Sarah was unable to get the woman out of her mind. For the rest of their holiday wherever they went, Sarah constantly looked behind her, jumping at her reflection in shop windows, wondering whether she would come face to face with her look-alike again.

She felt tearful and emotional, snapping at Brett for no obvious reason. In fact, for the first time in all the years she'd been visiting Highcliffe, she was pleased to get to the last day of her holiday, relieved to be going home.

'This isn't like you, Sarah,' Brett said. 'You're normally so strong, so positive. Don't let one little incident upset you.'

Back at home, Sarah didn't feel any better. She still felt unsettled by the encounter with the mystery woman. So, when three weeks later she found out the reason for her heightened emotions, the tears, the irrationality, everything seemed to fall into place.

'Pregnant!' Brett said, his face lighting up with excitement. 'How did that happen?'

Sarah laughed. 'I'm not really sure, but happened, it has. Are you pleased, Brett?'

'Pleased? I'm ecstatic,' he said, lifting her off her feet and twirling her around him.

Certainly, they hadn't planned to start a family just yet. They'd only recently finalised their plans to marry later that summer, but none of that mattered. Their friends and family were thrilled for them and their wedding went ahead as arranged, the only alteration being to the wedding dress that was let out slightly for Sarah's burgeoning bump.

'You know what you said about seeing that woman being an omen? I think you were right. It *was* an omen. Only a lucky one,' said Brett. 'Maybe that's what she was trying to tell us, that you were pregnant.'

'That's funny, because that was my first thought too. I'm so pleased as well. I didn't want to hold any bad feelings about Highcliffe. It's such a special place, one I hope our children will come to love as much as we do.'

Brett nodded in agreement. 'We'll have to take the baby there, maybe later this year. Show the sprog all the high spots.'

Sarah giggled. 'I'm sure it'll appreciate that.'

Some months later, their baby daughter arrived, with a shock of auburn hair, to match that of her mother's.

'She's beautiful,' said Brett, stroking her head for the first time. 'What should we call her.' He looked lovingly into his wife's weary face.

'How about Destiny?' she suggested, her eyes bright. 'After all, I'm sure fate took a hand in her arrival.'

'Mmm...' Sarah could see Brett mulling the thought over in his mind. 'Our little Destiny. That's absolutely perfect,' he said, a smile lighting up his face.

As it happened, Brett and Sarah didn't get to go back to Highcliffe that year. Or the following one. Their first few months, then years, as a family seemed to pass in a haze of dirty nappies and sleepless nights, only punctuated by occasional days out and weekends away with friends.

But with Destiny's third birthday approaching, Brett insisted that they needed a proper break away as a family. They managed to book into the same guest house that they'd stayed in the last time they'd visited and with Destiny now chatting endlessly, her eager anticipation of her first visit to the seaside made it all the more special for her parents.

As Sarah had always found, the sun shone unremittingly in Highcliffe and despite the advance of time, the town seemed to retain a nostalgic charm, reminiscent of a bygone age.

They spent their days rock pooling, Destiny in her red wellies endlessly fascinated by the creatures she found in her net. Then they would meander into town for a locally made ice cream, pausing to peer into the shop windows as they passed.

Sarah had never felt happier. They took photo after photo. Destiny in a rock pool, gleefully holding up some seaweed. Destiny on Brett's shoulders as he paddled into the sea. Destiny attempting her first clotted cream tea.

It was a holiday of magical memories and their final day in Highcliffe was no exception. They spent their remaining time on the beach, close to the water's edge, so Destiny could chase the gentle waves in and out under the watchful gaze of Sarah and Brett. Brett was a master sandcastle maker and endlessly patient as he made an elaborate fortress.

At the end of the day as the sun was going down, Sarah pulled on a white cheesecloth skirt and matching top to cover up her swimsuit. It was as she gathered up their belongings, packing away the buckets and spades and towels, that she heard the faint calling of her name.

'Sarah, Sarah,' the singsong voice called.

As her gaze scanned the beach, she saw in front of her, a little way out to sea, a woman dressed all in white. A feeling of nausea rose in her throat. It was the same woman she'd seen three years before in Highcliffe. Her doppelganger.

A cold chill ran through Sarah's body as the woman beckoned to her.

'Brett,' she cried, turning to grab his arm. But he was totally oblivious to Sarah and the woman in the water. His face was set in panic as he searched frantically around him.

'Where's Destiny?' he demanded, looking up and down the beach. 'I thought she was with you.'

Sarah's whole body turned cold. 'She was here a minute ago, just here. Making sandcastles. She can't have gone far. Destiny!' she called, fear ringing in her voice.

Brett and Sarah searched the sands in desperation, called

their daughter's name increasingly loudly until Sarah spotted, floating on the water's edge, a pink embroidered sun hat. Destiny's hat.

'No!' she cried. 'Not my baby, please not my baby.'

She waded into the sea, tears rolling down her cheeks, all the time calling out for Destiny.

Just then, as Brett returned flustered and breathless to their spot on the beach, having searched the area around them frantically asking anyone in his path if they'd seen a red-headed child, a small figure came running across the beach and flung her arms around her father's legs.

'Daddy, Daddy,' she cried. 'Are we going home now?'

'Oh, Destiny,' he sighed, relief flooding through his body. He scooped her up, pulling her closely to his side and showered her auburn hair with kisses.

'Where's Mummy?' she asked, looking around her.

Brett held Destiny tight in his arms as he looked all around him for his wife. He couldn't see in the distance the vision in white disappearing beneath the rolling waves.

'Sarah?' he called. 'Sarah! There's no need to worry, we've found her. Where are you, my darling?'

The House At Summer's End

by Helen M Hunt

The sun beat down on my head as I got off the bus on the long road that led to Summer's End.

I checked the crumpled piece of paper for the hundredth time. *The Manor House, Summer's End, Little Horton*, Noel's writing spidered drunkenly across the page.

I could almost smell the coffee as I remembered our first meeting in the café on the seafront. I'd never met anyone like him before, his long hair and tie-dyed clothes so out of place in our sleepy town. But after years of feeling bored and stifled, Noel was the key to my escape and the promise of something better and more exciting.

I hefted my suitcase up with both hands and started to struggle along the road. I hoped Noel hadn't forgotten he'd said I could come and stay at the Manor any time. As I started to sweat in the heat, I wondered if I was doing the right thing. Maybe turning up on the doorstep with all my possessions like some sort of refugee hadn't been what he'd had in mind.

I stopped and took some deep breaths to steady my nerves. Whether I'd done the right thing or not it was too late now, I'd burned my bridges at home. Finally pushed to the limit by my mother's fussing, I'd lost my temper the night before.

'I'm going somewhere I can get away from your constant nagging!' I'd shouted at her. 'It's 1970 not 1950, and you can't tell me what to do.'

She'd looked shocked at my outburst, but hadn't argued. So now I was here. All I needed to do was find Noel and explain.

'It's all very relaxed at the Manor House, Diana,' he'd told me as we shared coffee and he smoked Woodbines. 'Communal living, everything shared. There are no rules at Summer's End.'

And then he'd smiled in a way that made me feel like I was someone special.

As I arrived at the gates of the Manor, someone came out to greet me. She looked about my mum's age, but was jollier and dressed flamboyantly in a purple maxi-dress with her hair up in an orange turban. She made me feel like a scruffy child as I wiped my hands on my denim flares.

'Hello, I'm Xanthe. You look like you've come to stay,' she said.

'Yes, please,' I said. 'If I can.'

'Of course,' she said. 'Come into the house.'

Half way through drinking the cup of tea Xanthe made me I plucked up the courage to ask where Noel was.

'Bless you dear,' she said. 'Noel doesn't tell anyone where he is or when he's coming back.'

'But is it all right for me to be here? Noel said it was, but if he's not here...'

'No one needs to ask permission to be here,' she said. 'And Noel will be back when he's back, don't you fret.'

And so started my life at Summer's End. Without Noel, but with Xanthe and three other strangers.

Gisela from Germany had a room opposite the one that Xanthe allocated to me. She spoke perfect English, but kept herself very private and only showed up at mealtimes, when Xanthe would preside over the huge scrubbed pine table in the manor kitchen.

Then there was Dan. With dark hair and smoky eyes he seemed to spend most of his time either asleep or playing the guitar in his room. He was at the far end of the corridor and a cloud of joss sticks and patchouli oil hung outside his door.

Tall and muscular, Tom was in his early thirties and worked as a labourer on a local farm. He'd come back and strip off in the scullery every night, and the hairs prickled hotly at the back of my neck if I ever accidentally walked in on him.

Like Xanthe, the others accepted my presence without question. It was soothing and perplexing at the same time, but I was sure it would be fine when Noel arrived and explained to the others how he felt about me.

It was nearly a fortnight before he finally turned up.

'Hello Diana, do you want a cup of tea?' he said, as though he wasn't at all surprised to see me in the kitchen.

I opened my mouth to ask where he'd been, then remembered Xanthe's words about him coming and going as he pleased, and thought better of it.

'Two sugars, please,' I said and, with my heart thumping slightly, sat down at one end of the table.

'Are you settling in all right?' he asked me.

'Yes,' I looked down at the table, suddenly shy in his presence.

'That's good,' he said. 'Have you written to your family?'

'No.' I suddenly felt a stab of guilt about my mother. 'I sent her a postcard so she'd know I was safe. Do you think I should write?'

'That's not for me to say,' Noel said, running his fingers through his silver-streaked hair. 'There are no rules at Summer's End.'

Having Noel back seemed to bring us together, and that evening we all sat around the kitchen table long after the meal had ended. Noel opened a bottle of wine and poured a glass for each of us and Dan lit up a cigarette which filled the kitchen with sweetly-fragranced smoke. Tom looked more relaxed than usual, and Gisela's eyes sparkled with a life I'd never seen in them before. The wine seemed to loosen all our tongues and I wasn't surprised to see Noel starting a second bottle as Tom and Dan moved on to a Watney's Party Seven.

I almost said no as he came to top up my glass, but I didn't want to be the one who broke the spell of conviviality that had settled over us. So I kept drinking and let the mellow warmth of the wine flood through me. And when Noel refilled my glass again, I stopped counting and relaxed.

Darkness had long since fallen outside and owls were hooting in the trees when I noticed the conviviality was turning into something I wasn't sure I understood.

Dan was veering between looking sleepy and like he was about to burst out of his skin. Tom was slurring his words and seemed to be trying to pick a fight with his own shadow and Gisela was laughing unnaturally loudly when no one had made a joke.

Noel and Xanthe were having a conversation that seemed to exclude everyone else and he wasn't even looking at me.

As the night went on, I went from feeling accepted to feeling invisible.

For the first time since arriving at Summer's End I thought of my mum at home, drinking cocoa and listening to the wireless. Boring maybe, but at least there I'd known who I was. With a sick feeling I pushed away the thought that I wasn't special to Noel at all.

All the wine had made the room tilt at an alarming angle and I knew I had to get to bed. As I stood up, everything swayed and finally Gisela noticed I was struggling.

'You want to go to your room?' she asked.

I wouldn't have made it up the stairs without her arm to lean on, but I was relieved when she left me at my bedroom door and went soundlessly to her own room.

The next thing I knew I had woken up lying on my bed fully clothed, feeling sick and clutching my stomach. Suddenly I felt alone in the universe. Who were all these people at Summer's End anyway? They weren't my family and no amount of red wine would change that.

Tears flowed onto my pillow as I thought of my mum at home and I knew what I had to do. I had to go home straightaway. It didn't matter that it was the middle of the night.

One thing I was sure of though, despite my fuddled head and weak legs, I needed to tell Noel I was going. I rolled to the side of the bed and sat up.

Noel's room was down the far end of the corridor. I'd never been in there because Xanthe had impressed on me how much he liked his privacy, but I knew which one it was, so I gathered my dressing gown around me and set off towards it.

My steps were slow and deliberate as I tried to keep my head and my stomach on an even keel and I'd only made it about half way when a door opened and Tom appeared.

The sight of his bare chest made me lower my eyes, but this time I realised he wasn't wearing any trousers either. I tried hard not to look at him in his underpants.

'What are you doing?' he asked.

'I need to go home,' I said.

'Fine,' he said. 'But it's the middle of the night. You'll have to go in the morning.'

'No,' I said, my voice catching in the back of my throat. 'I need to go now. I want to tell Noel, he'll understand.'

'You can't go in Noel's room,' he said.

'Yes, I can. There are no rules at Summer's End.' I was sure of my ground as I repeated Noel's words.

I pushed past Tom and knocked on Noel's door.

'What's the matter?' called a voice from inside. Not Noel's voice, but Xanthe's.

I turned back to Tom and saw in his eyes that he'd known.

He caught my wrist and pulled me into his room.

'Surely you knew about Xanthe and Noel?' he said.

'No. I thought Noel was special, I thought...' my voice trailed off.

What had I thought? That Noel was in love with me? As I sat and shivered on Tom's bed I realised how stupid I'd been. Noel, Summer's End, all of it was an illusion.

Tom put his blanket around my shoulders and I lay on his bed next to him as sleep overtook me again.

The next morning, waking to daylight and birds singing, I felt awkward and embarrassed as I realised that no one at Summer's End cared whether I was there or not. They were all acting out a pantomime of their own choosing and would carry on just the same without me as an audience. Facing Noel and Xanthe would only add to my humiliation.

Tom seemed to read my mind. 'I'll walk you to the bus stop on my way to work,' he said. 'If you pack quickly we can leave before anyone else is awake.'

As we walked down the long expanse of road away from Summer's End, Tom asked what my plans were.

'I need to go back and see my mum,' I said, shivering in the morning breeze. I hoped I hadn't left it too late and that she would still want me back.

As Tom lifted my suitcase onto the bus I thanked him and felt brave enough to give him a brief kiss on the cheek. Of all the people I'd met at the manor he was the only one who felt real and regret tugged at me as I said goodbye to him.

But as the bus set off towards the coast I didn't look back. I'd followed my dream to Summer's End, but that's *all* it was. A dream. I stared out of the window as the fields full of crops rolled by. Summer would be over soon and I needed to go home before it started to get really cold.

Ghosts

by Karen Clarke

As I approach the house on the corner, my footsteps slow.

I pass the church, the pub and a primary school, digging my hands in my pockets to stop them shaking.

My therapist encouraged me to come here, an attempt to banish my ghosts, but I'm not so sure. Memories leap up, unbidden: things I've buried for years. But I guess that's the point.

I stop in front of a low brick wall and force myself to look at the house behind it. It's not the original. After the fire it stood empty for a while, and then new owners rebuilt it. There's no brick chimney or wooden porch and the old sash windows have gone.

In my nightmares, it had become a place of horror, with a crooked roof and rickety stairs, but I can see it's just an ordinary home and release my breath in a sigh.

Laying a hand on the gate – wrought iron now, not wooden with rusty hinges – I stare at the overgrown garden, alive with lupins, hollyhocks, and pink rhododendrons spilling out onto the drive.

Children's voices float on the air and I'm transported back in time, to me and my brother playing on the swing at the bottom of the garden, taking it in turns to push each other higher, convinced we can touch the clouds with our feet.

We were happy then, before Mum died and Dad...

Dad couldn't cope afterwards, and sent my brother to live with an auntie in Scotland. Billy emigrated when he grew up, and I haven't seen him for years. I sometimes wonder if he thinks of those days, or maybe like me he's tried to bury the past.

I used to wish I'd gone with him. Every day I prayed my father would change his mind and banish me too. It was as if the way I looked – so like Mum, with my curly tangle of dark hair and serious gaze – both drew and repelled him. It wasn't long until he couldn't stand the sight of me.

He never hurt me where it showed. He was clever like that. When the school introduced swimming lessons he stopped for a bit, and I was cautiously hopeful, and particularly helpful around the house, but it didn't last. He found other ways to hurt me instead. Ways I can't bear to recall.

'Can I help?'

I jump. The voice belongs to a woman, drying her hands on a tea towel. She's about my age, tall with an open expression and friendly smile.

'People often ask about the garden,' she says, gesturing at the riot of colour. 'I don't have to do much. Things seem to flourish in this soil.'

Probably the ash, I nearly say, and wonder if she knows the history. But the day is heavy with the scent of sweet-peas and it doesn't seem appropriate to bring it up.

'I used to live here,' I say instead, and her eyebrows go up a notch.

'Really?' She stares at me for a moment and I wonder if

I look as tense as I feel and try to soften my face. 'Why don't you come in?' she says, as if deciding I'm not a threat and the thought reassures me somehow.

'I don't want to disturb you.'

She shakes her head and says something about the school holidays, but my ears start ringing as I thrust open the gate, half expecting that when I walk through he'll be there, demanding to know where I've been, who I've been with and why his dinner isn't ready.

'...there's a lovely park down the road,' the woman is saying, and the day reasserts itself. Following her up the path, my heartbeat slowing, I glance at the house next door and think about Joe. Lovely Joe – my only ally back then.

He knew about Dad – heard him shouting one day, while he was out in the garden trying to train his new puppy, and he waited for me to come out later with the rubbish.

'You okay?' he'd said, his dark eyes anxious behind his glasses, the puppy tucked under his arm, and I'd stood there silently with tears on my face and he'd known without me saying a thing.

'Tell someone,' he urged one day, as we sat on the step with Binky between us, nibbling her paws, but I was too scared. Dad caught us talking and grounded me for a month, locking me in my room under the eaves every evening so I couldn't escape.

Joe told in the end and Social Services called round, but Dad was full of charm, like he was before Mum died, his eyes crinkling at the corners as he made them tea.

Seeing his face relax, I was filled with hope that he'd stay that way – that things might go back to normal and I smiled along too, and assured them everything was fine.

Things got worse afterwards and Joe stopped speaking to me, his face filled with sorrow whenever I caught his eye, but knowing he was there – that he cared – was like a lifeline.

'...room was too small, so we extended out the back.' The woman is leading me round like a tour guide, showing off her house which is airy and filled with light.

It bears no resemblance to the cramped, dark space I'd inhabited with Dad, our misery etched in the walls. The fire had cleansed it – erased the memories along with my father, and I'm glad it's a home filled with love.

Family photos line the shelves, and children's paintings clamour for space on the fridge. There's a pile of ironing in a wicker basket, with a cat perched on top and I smile, thinking how Mum would have loved that. She adored animals.

There's a shed at the bottom of the garden and my mind flickers back. Mum used to sketch in there, before she got sick – butterflies, usually, and once me and Billy on the swing, our faces lit up with joy. I still have it, worn soft with the years – the one thing Dad didn't destroy, because I kept it hidden.

I touch the door – newly painted – and for a split-second feel her presence. She was happy here. I thought I'd sense *him* – angry and toxic – and hadn't expected this. It's more than I'd hoped for.

'I bet you don't recognise the place,' the woman says as we walk back inside, her children trailing behind. I shake my head which feels lighter, as if it might float off.

'No,' I say, smiling, looking at the house next door. I can almost see Joe, standing at the upstairs window, watching over me. 'There are only good ghosts here.'

She frowns, her smile faltering.

'I'd better go,' I say shaking her hand, knowing I've unnerved her. 'Thanks for letting me look round.'

I close the gate softly and walk down the pavement, quickly this time, not looking back, my footsteps speeding up as I approach the car park.

I pull out my mobile and call my husband, knowing he'll be worried and wishing he'd insisted on coming up to the house with me.

'It's okay, Joe,' I say when he picks up, holding his breath with anxiety like he did that night, as we stood transfixed by the gate and watched the flames lick the sky.

Nobody questioned why my father lit candles before going to bed, and left them so close to the curtains; he was drinking heavily by then.

'Lucky Joe saw the smoke and got you out,' people said, unaware of my rucksack, neatly packed and hidden at the back of the shed. We'd been planning to run away together that night. 'Such a shame about your dad.'

But it wasn't a shame. It was the day my life began. Only later did the guilt crash in. I even blamed Joe for a while, for not stopping me – for giving me the candles.

'It's going to be okay,' I tell him again, more firmly this time, and hear him start breathing again.

The Girl in the Yellow Dress

by Bernadette James

The first time I saw her, on an otherwise unremarkable Wednesday in the gallery, I wasn't even sure that I'd seen anything at all. A flash of canary yellow caught my eye and then it was gone, leaving behind it a sense of something else, something feminine and beautiful.

I was too busy to stop and think about what I'd seen, or might have seen. It could have been anything or anyone or nothing and so I carried on chatting to the gallery customers, hoping that they would buy something and that the commission would bring me one step nearer to striking out on my own.

The second time, I was more certain. It was the yellow that did it. I'd always had an eye for colour and that particular shade, so vibrant yet with a velvety softness, was not something that the regular customers would wear. The men wore lounge suits in navy or charcoal grey, as I did, and the ladies were usually in black, with the more daring opting for red or imperial purple.

Yellow was a beach colour, a summer days colour, not appropriate for an evening at an upmarket art gallery. The yellow stood out against the morass of more typical colours and I was drawn to it, to see what kind of woman was prepared to make such a confident statement in such a traditional environment. By the time I'd made my way through the crowd she was gone.

I began to wonder whether I'd invented this person, desperate to bring some excitement into a life that had become monotonous. I knew that I was lucky to be surrounded by art, but it wasn't my art. Selling other people's work in someone else's gallery was supposed to be a stop-gap to pay the bills until I could make it as an artist myself, yet with every day that passed my dream seemed to move further away and become more of a fantasy. I had started to doubt whether I had it in me after all.

The girl in yellow was a welcome distraction and my mind had given her form, too. She was willowy, beautiful in an understated way, hazel eyes with a splash of green, blonde hair left to flow simply over her shoulders. I hadn't actually noticed any of this, yet it was how I saw her. And I knew that I would see her again.

The following week I was discussing a particularly dull landscape with one of the regulars who had taken a shine to it. I was close to a sale, one eye always on the room, when I saw her again. A fold of yellow fabric was just visible, the rest of it hidden behind one of the fake marble pillars. I made a hasty excuse and left, regardless of the sale, moving briskly through the people who had changed from being potential customers and had instead become obstacles in my path.

As I neared the pillar she had her back to me and turned at my approach. I stopped in amazement. She was exactly as I had imagined her. Exactly. She flashed a smile and then moved off. I started to follow her, but the customer had become restless and his hand on my arm checked my progress. When I looked up again, she wasn't there.

Each evening after that I watched for her, determined that this time she wouldn't get away. In the mornings, which I kept free for my own work, I tried without success to concentrate on the piece that I'd already started. All I wanted to paint was her. I put the first piece aside and tried to capture her essence on canvas. I was an artist after all, or trying to be, I should be able to do this, but she was just as elusive in paint as she had been in reality.

I saw her a few more times after that, a glimpse of yellow here, a flash of blonde hair there. She always left before I could speak to her. She knew that I had seen her, though, and often acknowledged me with a smile if I managed to catch her glance. And then, one day, when I'd given up hope, I sensed a presence behind me and there she was.

'Hello,' she said, her topaz eyes gleaming. 'We meet at last.'

'Do I know you?' I asked. 'Are you following me?' These were not the things I wanted to say. But although my mind was full of questions, these were the only ones that made any sense.

She laughed, a hearty, happy laugh.

'Yes,' she said, 'on both counts. I wanted to give you a chance, to see if you remembered.'

There was something in the look in her eyes, a joy of life that I knew I'd seen before. And the yellow...

'I'm sorry,' I said.

She held her hand out to me in a balled fist.

'This may help,' she said, and I reached out my open palm and she dropped something into it – a glass ball, with a centre of tiger's eye and green, just like her eyes. 'I thought it was time you had it back.'

All at once I was nine again.

'Is it you?' I asked.

'Yes, James,' she said. 'Yes, it's me.'

The playground was busy as always: gangs of boys kicking a ball against a wall; groups of girls giggling, discussing pop stars and dresses – even at that age. A smaller group was gathered in a corner watching a game of marbles. A child with a pudding basin haircut, wearing grey shorts and a grubby white shirt was challenging me for my best marble, a large glistening ball with a topaz swirl. I'd had it for years. I wasn't going to lose now. A deft flick and I had lost after all. As I looked up into the eyes of my conqueror I noticed for the first time how the marble matched them. Somehow I didn't mind so much then; it seemed right that she should own this thing that so closely resembled a part of her.

'You can have it back later,' she whispered, as we rose to go back to class.

'No, Cathy, you won it fair and square,' I replied and she glowed with pleasure that she could keep her prize with my blessing.

As we crossed the playground, the gaggle of girls began giggling.

'Hey, Cath,' the ringleader called out. 'Got something new for the party?'

Cathy ignored them, but I could see that her glow had faded. It was always the same for her.

She'd been at my school for a year now and her father had done his best since her mother had died. Despite this, hard times and three older brothers meant that there was no money for new clothes. Her head was always held high when she arrived at school in her brother's hand-me-downs and she played with the boys, laughed off the comments of the girls and stuck out her chin in defiance.

I had always admired her for that. She would have been my best friend, except that she was a girl, of course, and that wouldn't do.

Her tomboy ways suited her clothes, although I had sometimes wondered which had preceded the other. I couldn't remember ever seeing her in a dress.

As the day of the end-of-term party approached, the competition became fiercer and, for once, Cathy didn't seem quite so tough. She became more withdrawn, didn't want to play marbles or kick a ball, said she wasn't going to the stupid party anyway. I would notice her glance drifting over to the other girls and the light fade from her eyes.

I handed her the bag in break time the day before the party. I had made sure we were away from the others, over by the climbing frame where Cathy always won any challenges I gave her. She took it from me, not understanding, and reached in to remove its contents.

'It's not new,' I said, as she took out the yellow dress, complete with frills and spangles. 'It's too small for my sister now. She won't miss it.'

Cathy said nothing and for a moment I was worried that I'd offended her.

'I thought you could wear it to the party. If you don't like it...'

She stopped me with a glance.

'It's lovely,' she said. 'Thank you.' Then she put it back in the bag and we headed to class.

The next day Cathy arrived at school wearing the yellow dress. She had brushed her hair and had made a bow out of some ribbon and I had never seen anyone look so pretty.

As she passed the other girls, they all started laughing again.

'Dimwit!' they called. 'The party's not till this afternoon. You're supposed to get changed later.'

But she strode past them, straight to the climbing frame and started to swing from bar to bar, before joining us boys for a kickabout. Her grin nearly split her face.

'I told you, I don't want to go to the stupid party!' she called, laughing.

And I knew then that she was stronger and more beautiful than anyone I'd ever met or would meet again.

In the summer her family moved away and that was the last I saw of her, until now.

'You were the only one who was ever really kind to me,' she said. 'Because of you I learned who I was. I wanted you to know how happy I've been.'

'I'm glad,' I said, not quite believing that she was here.

She leaned in closer and for a moment I thought she would kiss me. Instead, she whispered in my ear.

'You have to be who you are, James,' she said.

She was half way across the room before I realised that she was leaving.

'Wait!' I called after her. 'The yellow! Do you always wear yellow?'

'Of course!' she called back and then she was gone.

I never saw her again. Although a part of me expected her to come back, the main part, the part that remembered her as she was, knew that it wasn't to be. Yet still every flash of yellow made me catch my breath: a child's balloon, a rose, the sun. They were all happy things, and I smiled as I exhaled. She had left me with that and also with something else that I was yet to discover.

As I stand in my gallery and scan the customers – my customers – I wonder where she is now. I have painted her a hundred or more times and it is those paintings that have made my name and are my most sought after pieces. I do paint other things as well, of course - not everyone wants a girl in a yellow dress on their walls - but they are the ones that created the publicity that bought me this gallery.

I did think she might get in touch when the pictures started making the television arts programmes. I'm sure she has noticed them and I can imagine her delight as she sees how I have portrayed her and how my face now wears a smile as broad as hers almost all of the time. That's what comes of being who you are meant to be.

But in my heart I knew that she'd done what she set out to do and she wouldn't be back. I had given her a gift many years ago and she had returned it to me. It was done. It was as it should be. We were never meant to be together. We were just meant to be happy.

And we are.

Previously Published

The following stories have been previously published:

Story	Publication
The One that Got Away	*Allas* (Sweden)
We'll Meet Again	*Take a Break Fiction Feast* (UK)
At Death's Door	*That's Life!* (UK)
	That's Life! (Australia)
From Tesco's With Love	*Best* (UK)
One Day at a Time	*Allas* (Sweden)
	That's Life! (Australia)
The Woman in White	*The Weekly News* (UK)
	Woman's Day (Australia)
The Girl in the Yellow Dress	*Allas* (Sweden)

About the Authors

Deborah Carr lives in Jersey with her patient husband, two teenagers and a grumpy Miniature Schnauzer. She spends most of her free time sitting on a pink, Lloyd Loom chair writing novels in her shed. As well as having previous work included in an anthology for the charity War Child, she's had a few pieces published in women's magazines in the UK, won a gold certificate for a short story in a local competition and has just finished her sixth novel. She blogs at debcarrs-daydreams.blogspot.com.

Karen Clarke is a writer and part-time library assistant. Her short stories have appeared in women's magazines in the UK, Australia and Sweden, and her first novel, *My Future Husband*, will be published by Random House in Germany in 2012. Karen lives in Buckinghamshire with her husband, three children and dog, and when she's not working, writing, reading, or messing about on the Internet, she remembers to update her blog at writewritingwritten.blogspot.com.

Sarah Dunnakey lives in West Yorkshire, where her day job is writing and verifying questions for TV quiz shows. Her story 'The Marzipan Husband' was broadcast on Radio 4 in July 2011. She has been placed or shortlisted in several short story competitions including second place in the 2011 Calderdale Prize, runner-up in the Fish Prize 2008 and winner of a WEA competition in 2008. Her work has also appeared in a number of short story anthologies. She has recently written her first novel.

Leigh Forbes has been writing since she could, and had produced a very short, very bad, novel by the age of eleven. Things have improved since then: after many years working on non-fiction, she began writing short stories in 2007, and has been published in *The Weekly News*, *The People's Friend*, and two anthologies. When she's not up some Scottish mountain in the fog, Leigh runs a web-development business and drinks coffee. She has a husband, three children, three bee hives, and Asperger's syndrome. She blogs at leighforbes.blogspot.com, tweets @writeleighso, and keeps a website at leighforbes.co.uk

Northamptonshire based writer **Helen M Hunt** writes short stories and features. Her short stories have appeared in a variety of women's magazines, and she regularly writes non-fiction for *Writers' Forum* and *Writing Magazine*. Helen also writes book reviews and runs the book review site *Bookersatz*. When she isn't writing she has a full time job looking after four cats. You can find out more about her, including details of her writing workshops and short story critique service, on her website: helenmhunt.co.uk.

Bernadette James was brought up in Cornwall and now lives in Surrey with her husband.

She has had numerous short stories published in women's magazines in the UK and overseas, and has won or been shortlisted in competitions for both poetry and short fiction, including shortlistings for the Bristol Prize, the Yeovil Literary Prize and the New Writer prize (under her real name of Sherri Turner). Her work has also appeared in several short story anthologies.

Helen Kara looks like a reasonably normal Englishwoman, but the inside of her is inhabited by several worlds and hundreds of characters.

Most of the time she hides this well, masquerading as a charity fundraiser by day and a sociable person by night. Yet she is never happier than when she has her feet up on the sofa, laptop open, and time to catch up with some of the people who live in her head.

Jenny Maltby was born in Jersey (the rock off the coast of France, rather than the newfangled American one), but has somehow ended up living in a medieval East Sussex village for the past ten years with her two teens and the smelliest dog in the county.

Having had non-fiction pieces and short stories published in *First Edition* magazine, *You're Not the Only One* and *Your Messages* anthologies, Jen is now working on a philosophical comedy novel. This largely involves staring out of the window, preoccupied with conversations between people who don't really exist. She blogs at twomoonstonight.com.

Kathleen McGurl lives by the sea in Bournemouth, and writes in the time remaining after slotting in a full time job, bringing up two teenage boys, and caring for a disabled mother. She has had dozens of stories published in women's magazines and is currently working on a historical novel, which grew out of an obsession with family history research Her blog, womagwriter. blogspot.com, aims to share information about the women's magazine fiction market and has proved popular with other writers.

Tamsyn Murray's New Year's resolution in 2008 was "to stop faffing about and take writing seriously". After a few false starts (or "rejections", as they're more commonly known), she sold her first short story to *My Weekly* in May that same year. Since then, her stories have been published in a number of women's magazines both in the UK and further afield. Having never really grown up, she quickly found her niche as a children's author, but still dabbles in the occasional short story and is "working" on an adult romantic comedy novel. One day, she might actually get further than typing "Chapter One"... Follow her on Twitter @TamsynTweetie or at tamsynmurray.co.uk.

Sally Quilford was born in South Wales, and now lives in the Peak District with her husband and four westies. She is a columnist for *Writers Forum* magazine, and has also had countless stories and articles published in magazines in Britain and abroad.She is the author of seven *My Weekly* Pocket Novels. You can find out more about Sally at sallyquilford.co.uk.

Jill Steeples loves writing short stories, particularly those with a twist in the tail, and her work has appeared in popular women's magazines in the UK, Scandinavia and Australia. She was a contributor to four of the *Sexy Shorts* charity anthologies published by Accent Press and the more recent 'Diamonds and Pearls' anthology. She's currently working on a romantic novel, and was a finalist in the 2011 Mills & Boon New Voices Competition. She lives in Leighton Buzzard with her husband, two teenage children and mad English Setter.

Cally Taylor lives in Bristol with her boyfriend and baby son, and their ridiculously large DVD/book/music collection. She shares her "study" with the washing machine and a surf board, and writes her novels in any spare moments she can squeeze in between the day job and her social network addiction. She started writing fiction in 2005 and her short stories have won several awards and been published by a variety of women's magazines including *My Weekly*, *Take a Break Fiction Feast* and *Woman's Own*. Her debut novel *Heaven Can Wait* has been translated into 13 languages and was voted "Debut Novel of the Year" by chicklitreviews.com and chicklitclub.com. Her second novel, *Home for Christmas*, was published by Orion in November 2011. You can find out more about Cally by checking out her website at callytaylor.co.uk.

4655725R00104

Printed in Great Britain
by Amazon.co.uk, Ltd.,
Marston Gate.